SUBMISSIVE SEDUCTIONS

Also by Christine d'Abo

30 Days

SUBMISSIVE SEDUCTIONS

Christine d'Abo

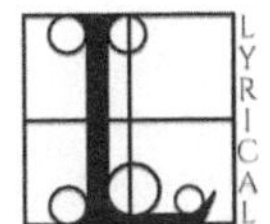

LYRICAL PRESS
Kensington Publishing Corp.
www.kensingtonbooks.com

Earlier versions of "Dom for Sale" and "Training the Dom" were published by Ellora's Cave in 2013.

LYRICAL BOOKS are published by

Kensington Publishing Corp.
119 West 40th Street
New York, NY 10018

All Kensington titles, imprints, and distributed lines are available at special quantity discounts for bulk purchases for sales promotion, premiums, fund-raising, educational, or institutional use.

Special book excerpts or customized printings can also be created to fit specific needs. For details, write or phone the office of the Kensington Sales Manager: Kensington Publishing Corp., 119 West 40th Street, New York, NY 10018. Attn. Sales Department. Phone: 1-800-221-2647.

Lyrical Press and the Lyrical Press logo Reg. U.S. Pat. & TM Off.

eISBN-13: 978-1-60183-474-4
eISBN-10: 1-60183-474-8
First Electronic Edition: February 2016

ISBN-13: 978-1-60183-475-1
ISBN-10: 1-60183-475-6
First Print Edition: February 2016

Printed in the United States of America

PART 1

DOM FOR SALE

CHAPTER 1

I'm still not entirely sure what possessed me to say yes when Connie asked me to attend the charity auction at her BDSM club. I mean, this was all new to me and I really didn't have a fucking clue about the lifestyle or if I actually wanted what I *thought* I wanted. But all of the proceeds were going to support a suicide hotline, to which she damn well knew I would say yes. And, really, it was the best chance I had to give this a go, yank my fantasies into the daylight. Or spotlight, in this particular instance.

Buy a Dom for a night.

Rent a man and get him to take control, all in the safe confines of a club with people who knew what they were doing.

A hard chance to pass up.

Still, I had to question myself: What the hell was I thinking? It's not like I knew who any of these people were, or what was truly expected of me. How could I honestly walk in there and offer myself up like the proverbial lamb to a man whom I didn't know the first thing about?

So, the plan in my head had been to go and watch, take some notes, and figure out if this was really what I wanted. What harm was there in watching, right?

So naïve.

In typical Connie fashion, she wasn't about to let me sit on the sidelines. Oh no. I should have anticipated my best friend's need to meddle.

Connie had told me there wasn't a dress code. *No, Liz, you don't have to get all fancy. Not really. Go as you are and you'll be fine. Just shave and pluck, put on some of that nice jasmine vanilla cream of yours, and the men will eat you up. Maybe wear the new Diesel jeans, they show off your ass. Oh, and here's a nice corset!* I had no doubt she thought she was being comforting, supportive even. What she actually did was make me even more nervous about going than I was in the first place.

I had put on the Diesels and a midnight blue corset I'd picked up a few months ago. The coloring went well with my blond hair and pulled in my slightly thick waist. I hoped the outfit would be enough for me to blend into the crowd. I didn't want to stick out like the obvious newbie I was. Connie had emerged from her room wearing PVC and stilettos high enough to have *my* calves screaming for relief. She looked like a Dom's wet dream. I'm surprised Stephen let her out in public without him, looking like that. It also served to remind me how completely out of my element I was about to be.

Before I'd been able to turn tail and hide in a corner of our apartment, she grabbed my arm and hauled me to the club.

Arriving at the Tail Whip was a bit of a shock to the system. There were lines and lists and bouncers to get through—the club was closed to only members and guests, which I found reassuring. Even with our names on the list and our invitation in hand, I have to say the third degree that the bouncer put us through would have chased me away under normal circumstances.

Not that it killed my nervous excitement in the least.

Clearly I was a sucker for punishment after all.

The club building was pretty much a converted warehouse. The rafters were exposed and lights dangled from long chains. The walls were concrete blocks, painted in an array of blues, grays, and blacks. I knew there wasn't any alcohol, so I was surprised to still see a bar tucked off in the corner. The main area had a large stage, and it looked like the organizers had thrown up some makeshift curtains to hide the participants.

The majority of the patrons had on even less than Connie. You'd think it was the people in the crowd up for bid and not those on the stage. I would have fit in better if I'd hauled off my corset and put electrical tape over my nipples like that woman over there. Damn, that was going to hurt coming off. Maybe.

"You're a bitch," I hissed as she pulled me toward the front. "I look like an idiot."

"You look fine, Liz. It's not like you're a member yet. Besides, some of the Doms like an understated image. More than a few, in fact." I should have known then that she'd been planning something. She had that wild look in her eyes that she got when Stephen was about to come over to play.

"Not that it will matter." I tugged up the top of my corset before rocking up on the tips of my boots to see over the naked shoulder of the man standing in front of me. "I can't see me getting a Dom. At least not a good one with what I can afford." My luck I'd end up with a first-time Dom and the two of us would do nothing but stand around and stare at each other. "I'm still not sure I even want to do this."

I had limited money to spend on things that weren't bills. The new job with Schultz Associates was, well, still new, and I had student loans to pay back and a future house to save for. Shelling out a couple hundred dollars for what essentially amounted to a rent-a-date seemed pretty irresponsible. And desperate. I wasn't desperate.

Well, maybe sort of desperate.

Wiping my hands down the front of my jeans, I hoped I didn't look as nervous as I felt. I didn't think Doms would necessarily want someone who they thought would freak out at the first sign of a whip.

"I told you, I'll chip in. You'll win one of them tonight. Trust me." There it was again, that glint that told me Connie was up to no good.

She was my best friend in the whole wide world, and the only person I knew who was a sexual submissive. It was one of the things that had caught my attention at college, how she would home in on particular men, sometimes the ones I wouldn't expect, and take them home. It wasn't until we became roommates during our second year that I realized exactly what she did with them once she got them home.

I'd bought earplugs early on. Then I quickly misplaced them.

I'd masturbated so many nights listening to Connie and her Doms, I'd never be able to admit it to her. It wasn't that I was turned on by them—it was the sounds, the tones, the glimpses of red skin I'd see on her body the next day.

When she'd eventually settled down with Stephen, things changed with her. It was fascinating to watch Connie change from the wild girl looking for a hot time to the devoted girlfriend who got off on having her man spank her ass.

I knew I was jealous of what Connie and Stephen had. What I could never be sure of was if it was the spankings that were so appealing, or the idea of finally having someone I loved be so intimate with me.

The crowd around us continued to buzz with excitement, growing in noise and size as we got closer to go live time. I tried hard not to stare at the press of bodies around me. Most were in varying degrees of nakedness and all seemed aroused. There were a few people who I assumed were Doms scattered throughout. It was surprisingly easy to pick them out and not because of the clothing they wore. They had an air to them that was unmistakable. A confidence, bordering on arrogance in some cases, that rolled off them in waves.

Those were the ones I looked at, studied with my sidelong glances. The women looked powerful, like they could be running a large corporation, or be cops, anything that required power and control. My gaze didn't linger as long on them. I was straight—well, for the most part. I wouldn't kick a beautiful woman out of bed, but I didn't think I was ready for something like that.

No, my eyes were on the guys.

"I don't have a clue whom to bid on." God, this was weird, like considering what cut of meat to buy at the market. While it wasn't as frenzied as Tina's bachelorette party we'd gone to last month, there was certainly less clothing. Not that I have an issue with nakedness, I'm just not used to seeing it in such abundance. "I'm not you. I feel like such a fake here."

Connie sighed and draped an arm around my shoulders. "Don't be an idiot. You're fine. Now, they'll be starting soon. Don't do anything about bidding until I tell you to. Just watch and learn."

It was odd, being at an event like this. This wasn't a part of who I was, the public displays and flaunting of sexuality. I worked in an office, at a desk. I flirted with my married boss because he's old enough to be my dad and is of the generation where it's not taken seriously. I don't bid on men with the intent of asking them to tie me up, spank me, and make me scream before they make me come.

The MC stepped out onto the middle of the stage, a microphone in hand and a grin fixed on his face. He was wearing tight leather pants, but no top. His nipple piercings glinted in the spotlight. Umm, ouch. Maybe ouch? I'd have to ask Connie.

"Good evening, ladies and gentlemen. Welcome to our Third Annual Auction for Hope. All proceeds tonight will benefit the local suicide hotline."

I clapped along with everyone else and did my best to ignore the tingling starting up in my legs. This didn't have to be about me at all. I was simply here as a willing supporter of a good cause. There was no reason to focus on the possibility that I might find a Dom here tonight. Someone to help me relax and get my head straightened out.

"Tonight we have some of our club favorites ready and willing for you to buy them!" The crowd erupted in cheers and catcalls. Bodies bumped into me and I could have sworn someone grabbed my ass.

"Now, now, settle down." The MC wagged his finger at the crowd. That only served to jack the excitement further. "If you don't behave, we won't get to play."

Connie started laughing. "Christian is eating this shit up tonight."

"Who is he?" It would figure Connie knew the man.

"He's one of the bouncers for the club. A big old sub if you can believe it."

No. Way.

I looked the man over again, but there was no way I would ever have guessed the buff, jovial man strutting about the stage was a sub.

"Is he gay?" I turned to look at Connie. "Not that it matters."

"Straight as a board, our Christian. He likes his women in control, though I don't think he's found one yet to his liking."

If there was any chance I was a Domme, I would have jumped at the opportunity to be with a guy like him. But the one thing about my sexuality I was certain of was that I didn't like to take charge between the sheets. Or on the couch.

Anywhere, really.

Christian leaned forward. "Are you ready to get this party started?" Cheers exploded around me. "I can't hear you." Another roar from the crowd, this one deafening. "Excellent! Then here we go!"

When the first person came out onstage the crowd around us pulsed with excitement. It was enough to send a shiver through me, stopping somewhere in my pussy. The scent of arousal wasn't one I'd ever encountered on such a strong level before. Like being hot boxed at a concert and unintentionally getting high, I felt my body responding to the incidental touches from those around me. The cardboard number card grew sweaty in my hands as I watched the first sub come onto the stage.

I don't know what I'd been expecting, but she didn't look weak or scared. The woman, who looked to be several years older than myself, walked with purpose to the front, clasped her hands together, and lowered her gaze. She was in excellent shape, most of her body not hidden by the PVC halter top and skirt she wore.

She wasn't the only one either. Some of them were confident, a few cocky. All of them were beautiful, especially when the Doms in the crowd came to claim their prizes. I got so wet at the sight of them being led off the stage, some by leashes, others by the hand or wrist, all going willingly to experience something I had only imagined before.

After a solid twenty minutes, Christian came back out onstage, still grinning. I wondered if he ever stopped. "I know you're going to be disappointed, but that was our last submissive for the night."

"We want you, Christian!"

The crowd laughed and even I couldn't help but chuckle. Christian for his part pointed in the direction of the voice and made a *tsking* noise in the mic. "Not tonight, my lovely. Poor Christian has work to do."

The rumble of disappointment was easy to feel.

"We'll take a short break and then it will be time for the Doms. Get your cards ready."

Connie was practically bouncing in her stilettos as she chatted with a few people around us. I probably should have at least made an attempt to join in the conversation, but at this point I was starting to freak. The Doms were next, which meant I really had to make a decision on whether or not I was actually going to do this. It's not like Connie was forcing me to be here. She wouldn't get mad at me if I tore up the number card currently clutched in my hand and ran screaming out of the club.

She might, however, be a bit disappointed that I wimped out after she'd gone to such lengths to get me an invitation to the event. The last thing I wanted to do was disappoint her.

Better to do this. Worst case I could simply take the Dom with me to a local coffee shop and have a conversation with him. I mean, what better way to figure out if this is something that I could be into than to have an extended chat with a man who saw to the pleasure of others?

The tension in my shoulders lessened as I made my decision. There really was no pressure beyond what I was putting myself under. I scanned the stage to see if Christian was about to come back out when the movement of the stage curtain caught my attention. There was a man standing on the other side scanning the crowd. He was clearly checking out the audience, and from the slight frown on his face I don't think he liked what he saw. When his gaze landed on mine, I instantly felt myself blush.

Damn.

He stopped frowning.

His hair looked black in the dim light and I couldn't make out his eye color from this distance. Not that the details matter because he was simply the most attractive man I'd ever laid eyes on. Completely out of my league. He frowned again and for a moment I thought he might turn around and disappear back behind the curtain. Instead, he pulled the curtain back a bit farther so I was better able to see the rest of him.

God, he wasn't just handsome, he was fucking gorgeous.

Looking away, I really did focus my attention on Connie and her friends then. There was something intense in that man's gaze that unsettled me down to my very core. I didn't like the butterflies that had decided to take up residence in my stomach, or how I knew he'd been the reason they were there.

Thankfully, it wasn't much longer before Christian came back out on the stage. It was impressive how quickly he managed to work the crowd up. Over the break there'd been a bit of a shift of the crowd, some of the Doms had moved away to be replaced by people who I assumed to be subs. The competition was going to be fierce.

"Ladies and gentlemen, we are ready to rumble once more. This time, it's Doms on parade!"

Shit. I took a deep breath and got ready.

Connie grabbed my arm and gave me a squeeze. "Okay, here we go."

"I'm not sure how much to spend." What the hell was it worth to spend a night figuring out fundamentally who you were? I don't think you can actually put a price tag on something like that.

"I told you not to worry about the money. Plus, I have a plan."

"Connie." I know I was whining, but I'd been on the receiving end of her plans on more than one occasion. They usually ended up with stains on my clothing and several bruises.

"Shut up." Connie grinned. "Don't vote on this first one. Or even the second. I'm waiting for someone particular to come up." Connie squeezed my bare arm, her blood red nails digging into the skin. "He'll be worth every penny."

"Had him before?" Taking my best friend's castoff wasn't something I'd had in mind when I'd agreed to come tonight.

"Well, kind of. He's a friend of Stephen's and we've hung out a lot over the past few months. I've done a scene with both of them once. Just trust me, okay. Gareth's perfect for you." Normally, trust wasn't an issue between us, so I was willing to roll with it for the time being. God help her if he turned out to be some sort of weirdo.

I'm not sure what Connie's definition of perfect was, but the three men who came ahead of the man she had in mind would have been pretty fucking amazing as far as I was concerned. They were fit and attractive and I had no doubt they could rock my world. So what if one of them had more piercings than me, the second looked like he belonged in a biker gang, and the third . . . were those vampire teeth?

Okay, I was going to trust her after all.

When Connie grabbed my arm again and bounced, a nervous rush pounded through me that set my skin tingling. Christ, I was really going to do this. With the man my best friend thought was perfect for me.

It was the man from behind the curtain.

I probably should have been paying attention to the announcer going on about Master Gareth's specialties, his background as a Dom, that he worked at a university, had a PhD, blah, blah, blah. I normally have a great head for details and can pull them up at a moment's notice. The only thing I could focus on was the intense look in his eyes as he scanned the crowd.

What the hell was I getting myself into?

Now that he was out in the open, I couldn't help but further appreciate his appearance. He was tall, at least six feet, if not over, and his brown hair was long enough to look stylish, without falling into the messy category. He hadn't shaved, so he had the sexy scruff look going on. The tight T-shirt he wore did little to hide the very fit body lurking beneath, and his leather pants looked sculpted to his legs.

Unlike the others, Master Gareth was someone I would feel comfortable going out to supper with, or bringing home to meet my mom.

Hah! I could hear that conversation now. *Hi, this is Gareth. Yeah, we met at a BDSM club. Pass the potatoes, please?*

Not that I had any plans beyond buying him for a night of fun.

Or even having a conversation.

I was still debating that last point.

I doubt he could actually see much of anything given how bright the spotlight was, but for a moment when his gaze swept past where I stood, I swear he hesitated. Maybe he was remembering where I'd been standing from before. Why the hell would he even care?

"Ladies, Master Gareth can promise you a night of passion, control, able to push you to your limits." Christian pointed at the crowd. "Remember, all the proceeds go to the suicide hotline. We'll start the bidding at one hundred dollars."

I'm pretty sure Connie was the one who lifted my arm holding the bidding card. She held it up for several minutes until the competition started to fall to the wayside and my courage to keep going kicked in. Someone dimmed the stage lights and I knew the second his eyes adjusted and he could see me. Christ, we were so close to the front of the stage, me below him looking up, he felt like a giant or a god passing judgment over me.

My pussy clenched at the thought of what he could do if we were alone.

"The bid goes to number one thirty-nine for five hundred dollars." Christian nodded at me and for the first time it looked like my dreams might actually come true.

"Six hundred!" A voice from the side of the room shouted, eliciting a soft *ooooh* from the crowd.

I'm not prone to violence, but I was ready to jump over and punch whoever that woman was. The bitch.

I let my hand drop.

"What are you doing?" Connie hissed and jerked my arm back up. "Six hundred and ten!"

"I can't afford that." Well, I could, but things would be tight for the next while. No extra lattes for me.

"I told you I'd help."

"Six hundred and twenty." The woman sounded far too chipper.

I looked up once more at Master Gareth and couldn't hold back a sigh. This was crazy. There were better ways to explore one's sexuality without skipping groceries for the next month. I would have turned to Connie then and, good cause or no, bowed out. I would have if Master Gareth hadn't taken that moment to look into my eyes and cock an eyebrow.

Shocking how much a person could say without speaking a word.

I shrugged. What the hell did he expect? I couldn't afford to let things go too far.

Could I?

Master Gareth smirked.

Shit.

"The bid is six hundred and twenty-five to you, miss." With Christian's proclamation, every eye in the room turned to me. I shivered at the attention. Master Gareth snorted loud enough for me to hear him.

Bastard.

"Seven hundred." The words left my mouth before I gave my brain a chance to process them. Holy crap, I'd gone insane. Absolutely stark raving mad.

I managed to hold Master Gareth's gaze long enough to hear Christian shout, "Sold!" before I let it fall to the floor. That was the right thing, wasn't it? No eye contact? What the hell was I doing? *Gah!* At least the hotline would have a good month.

"Come here." I jumped when I realized it was *him* talking to me and not Christian.

To me.

Tall, strong Master Gareth.

I didn't need Connie's shove to get moving, though it did help to point me in the right direction. She'd shoved a handful of bills into my pocket, but I was too freaked out to look at that point. Somehow I made it onto the stage and stumbled across the black floor until I was beside him. The lights were bright and even a bit hot once I'd stood still. His cologne was musky, and yet there was a hint of something very male behind it.

It didn't seem right to lead him away, so I stood there and waited. The other subs had taken the lead, but right then my brain was misfiring and it was all I could do not to fall over on my face.

"Time to pay." His words were spoken softly but held the authority I'd secretly been craving.

Looking up at him, I was stunned to see there was a lot of humor lurking in those brown eyes of his. It would be easy to lose myself in them, stare until I forgot myself. When he reached out and squeezed my hand, I jumped. "They're waiting over here."

"I hope they take credit." I muttered the words, barely loud enough for myself to hear. Master Gareth chuckled and I melted even more.

His hand wrapped around my wrist and I was tugged offstage, the cheers and catcalls of the crowd chasing behind me. Master Gareth led me toward a desk off the stage along the side wall close to the bar. Some birdlike woman shoved a number of forms under my nose and instantly launched into a monologue of dos and don'ts.

I briefly remember seeing a waiver, something resembling a release form, and other bits to ensure I wouldn't come back and sue them if things didn't go the way I wanted. I did my best to focus on the sheets and make sure I knew what I was signing. Not that I was impulsive by nature, but given what I'd gotten myself into tonight, God only knew what would happen.

"How will you be paying for tonight, dear?" The woman's too-large eyes blinked at me like she was expecting me to run away any second.

I hated that my hand shook as I reached into my pocket and pulled out what Connie had shoved in there.

Then I gasped.

There were five one-hundred-dollar bills with a Post-It note attached: *Love Connie and Stephen.* I handed the money over, trying to think of a way I could possibly repay them, and pulled out the single blank check I'd shoved into my jean's front pocket. "I can postdate this, right?"

"Oh yes, darlin'. I suspect you won't be alone."

I couldn't imagine why Connie and Stephen would go through all this to give me a night with a Dom. I mean, we're good friends and all, but five hundred dollars is a shit-ton of cash for anything. But if they also knew Master Gareth, then there might be something more going on than I knew.

As I filled out the information, along with another sheet promising them my firstborn if the check bounced, I was aware of Master

Gareth standing to my side. I could feel his gaze traveling down my body, the weight of it pausing on my ass. He was even more attractive up close and personal than he'd been half shrouded behind the stage.

I shifted my stance, thrusting my hip to the side. Not that I was preening. No, I wouldn't do that. If he was an ass-man and was taking the time to look in the first place, then who was I to deny him a quick gander? I wasn't sure if I imagined the soft hum of pleasure coming from him. Maybe it was simply wishful thinking that he had a thing for asses that had a bit of extra padding on them.

The urge to giggle clawed up my throat and threatened to explode. God, I didn't want him to think I was some sort of crazy freak who lost it over paperwork. Sucking in a breath, I forced my attention back on the forms in front of me.

My back ached slightly as I stood and held out the sheaf of papers along with my payment to bird-lady. "There you go. Holler if I've forgotten anything."

"I'm sure it's fine, dear. Now, Master Gareth, if you want to use the Blue Room it's available for you."

I didn't see him nod and yet, I could tell he had. It was the same way I knew he stepped away and expected me to follow him. I probably should have jumped right away, but something held my feet in place, preventing me from trailing behind him like a puppy.

Oh yeah, I knew that feeling. It was terror.

I'd forgotten how big a chicken I really was.

"We don't have to, if you'd prefer something else." I snapped my gaze up to his at the sound of that wonderfully deep voice. Like his eyes, I think it would be very easy to get lost in it. I knew then if I asked, I could arrange to meet him another night. We could do drinks over at the bar and then I'd have a chance to do some more reading. . . .

"There is a coffee shop—" He inclined his head toward the club's front doors.

"No!" Wow, that came out a bit more forceful than I'd intended. I licked my lips, surprised at how dry my mouth had suddenly gotten. Master Gareth was smirking now and a small part of me hated him for it. "The Blue Room is fine."

God have mercy on me.

CHAPTER 2

I had to take a moment to calm my nerves before I could even attempt to follow him. And while there wasn't any rule stating anything had to happen tonight, I'd just bought an evening with him and it would be a shame not to take advantage.

Honestly, I'd done my fair share of research already. This wasn't a new fantasy for me. And despite Connie's moaning, I didn't go on and on about wanting to find a guy to dominate me in the bedroom. I hadn't peppered her with questions about what it felt like to be tied up, spanked, fucked with a dildo while you sucked your boyfriend off.

Okay, I might have asked a few questions once or twice.

Maybe a dozen . . .

Master Gareth stopped at the opening to a hallway. He didn't turn back to face me, but I knew he was waiting. There would be no one to force me into this. The charity would happily take the money regardless of whether I took advantage of my purchase or not. And I'm sure Master Gareth would easily step back up onstage to find another bidder. No one cared if I didn't take this golden opportunity to explore something that had been haunting me for years. This was all down to me.

I let out a huff, straightened my shoulders, and walked toward him.

When I reached him, Master Gareth turned his face so his profile was clear over his shoulder. "The Blue Room is this way."

I knew he was giving me a chance to change my mind, to turn

around and leave. Not surprising given my hesitation in coming even this far. I would have said it was sweet, but he didn't come across as the sweet type. Plus I knew if I didn't do this now and walk away, I'd regret it.

"I'm right behind you."

"Sir." There was something about the way he said that single syllable that made me shiver. It was that same feeling deep down that I'd experienced when I'd first caught sight of him behind the curtain. "From this point on you are to address me as Sir."

"Yes, Sir." Oh, shit. Shit, damn, holy hell.

He moved then and somehow I was able to follow, keeping a respectable distance behind. The gap gave me opportunity to ogle his ass, which was tight, muscular, and encased in leather. Maybe that was the appeal of the BDSM lifestyle. Leather. It smelled wonderful, primal, felt amazing when I'd run my hands along it.

No, there was more to it than that.

I nearly ran into him when he slowed to let another couple pass us in the hall. He turned his head, quirked his eyebrow once more, and I knew I'd been caught. Well, what did he expect? He had a nice ass.

It didn't take us long to get where we were going. Master Gareth stopped in front of a door, his hand on the handle. He looked at me again, but this time there was no humor in his gaze. "When we go in, I want you to take the seat that you find inside and place it in the center of the room. Then we are going to have a little chat. Understand?"

A chat? Not exactly what I thought we'd be doing. And why the hell was the idea of having a *conversation* so fucking arousing? I must have been more hard up than I'd thought.

"Yes, Sir." I wondered if he could hear the pounding of my heart in my chest. It shouldn't be that difficult given how hard it was beating. God, I think it might have rivaled the dance music that I normally listened to.

His lips twitched into that smirk of his once more. Instead of being infuriating, it was starting to appeal to me. I wondered what else I could do to make him smile? Master Gareth opened the door with a quick twist of the handle and stepped aside to let me past.

The room was surprisingly empty of things that I would have suspected present in a BDSM club. There were rings positioned on the back wall and a small wall unit in the corner. Besides the chair he'd already mentioned, that was it. No large crosses, or swings, no contraptions of any kind. Not even a window or mirror for others to see in or for me to check out how red my skin would look.

I didn't want to admit to being disappointed, but there was a small part of me that felt like a kid after the Christmas presents had all been opened. Master Gareth cleared his throat and I realized that I was still standing in the doorway. I quickly strode over to the chair, picked it up, and awkwardly carried it to the center of the room. The damn thing was heavy.

I sat down even though he hadn't mentioned that being a part of the plan. I assumed, even though that tended to get me into trouble, the intent of the chair was for me to use it, not simply stand beside it. He appeared to be the logical type. Rubbing my hands along my jeans, I let out a shaky breath and waited for what was to come next.

Time ticked on for what felt like hours, when, in fact, it must have been only heartbeats. Master Gareth stared at me long enough for the hair on the back of my neck to prickle and a tingle to start somewhere in my toes. It was unnerving and unnatural to be under such intense scrutiny by one person. Me! I'd always been more of a fade into the background type than one to stand out in the spotlight. The way his gaze slipped over my body was almost too much.

He hummed softly before moving into the room and quietly closing the door. As far as I could tell there was no lock, which meant I could leave at any time. Reassuring. He slapped his hand against the side of his leg and looked at me long and hard. I don't know what I was expecting him to do when he finally did move, but him coming to squat down in front of me, his forearms resting on his knees, wasn't it.

God, he had sexy arms.

"Hi." He had a great voice, too. It was deep the way I liked it, gravelly. I hoped he didn't smoke. "Now, I know you paid for tonight, but there are a few things we need to discuss before I go any further. This is for my benefit as much as yours. Okay?"

Oh. I hadn't thought he'd need any time to get ready to do something. Maybe my first instinct about taking it slow was correct after all and we were only going to make plans to do this another time, or not do anything at all and simply talk. I was okay with that.

I was.

Well, I'm sure I could work my way into it if I had to.

"Hi." I smiled, though my cheeks twitched. They did that when I was nervous or had to pose for family photos. "I'm Liz."

"You're a friend of Connie's." It was a statement and not a question, so he'd clearly recognized her out in the crowd by me. He held out his hand for me to shake. It was a nice hand, large and warm. Everything about him seemed warm and inviting. Not exactly the image I'd had for a Dom. "I haven't seen you at the club before."

"No, this is my first time. Connie finally convinced me to come." I really didn't want to let go of him, but it would have been weird to keep the handshake going much longer. It was nice when, instead of returning his hand to dangle between his legs, he placed it on my knee.

"Is Liz short for Elizabeth?"

"No, actually. My mom figured everyone would call me Liz anyway so she said she saved me a step." I laughed. Mom would die if she knew I'd mentioned her in a sex club. She'd die knowing I was even *in* a sex club. More things I'd have to keep to myself. "I always laugh when people call me Elizabeth."

"So, why are you here, Liz?" He'd started rubbing small circles with his thumb on the inside of my knee. It felt like there was a direct line from that single spot connected to my cunt. Those most intimate of muscles clenched and I was shocked at how aroused I'd gotten in such a short time.

He'd asked me a question? Oh, right. I licked my lips once more and tried to smile again. My lips were still twitching.

"I'm here . . . because I'm curious."

"About what?" he asked when I didn't continue. He was perceptive, which I guess shouldn't have surprised me. "There are many things you could be wondering about. If I don't know specifically what they are, then I can't help you."

This time I couldn't stop the giggle from escaping. "Sorry."

"What do you have to be sorry for?" He squeezed my knee and for some reason that helped me relax.

"For being a bit freaked out. This isn't what I expected tonight would be like." He wasn't at all like the Dom I'd pictured in my head. In so many ways he was much better.

"How so?" The glint was back in his eyes and I could tell he was at least seeing the humor in the situation as much as I was.

"First, a distinct lack of nudity." I shifted in my chair, but not enough to break his touch. "Honestly, I didn't think there would be this much talking. Connie never mentioned that there would be talking." To be fair to her, she didn't say much of anything. She'd always believed in experience being the best teacher.

Master Gareth cocked his head to the side and frowned for a moment. "You're a stranger to me. I don't know what your limits are, your likes or dislikes. I'm also a man with a certain amount of pride. I hate failing to live up to expectations."

"I guess I can appreciate that."

"I'm a stranger to you as well, Liz. One who will end up having you in some compromising positions. I think taking a few moments to have a conversation and get to know each other would be prudent. Don't you?"

"Yeah, that makes sense." Smart, sexy, *and* dominant.

I totally ignored the part of my girl brain that perked up and wanted to ask for his phone number. Because buying him for a night was all well and good, but starting to think about the possibility of having a relationship with him went well beyond what I should be considering just then. I could tell he was calm, where I tended to bounce through life. It would do me some good to find a person like him.

"Liz, can you look at me?"

I hadn't even realized I'd broken eye contact. Connie always teased me that it was the biggest sign that I was a natural submissive. Get me in the room with a dominant man and I'm incapable of seeing higher than someone's knees. I found it infuriating; she thought it hilarious.

Master Gareth had beautiful eyes, so why wouldn't I want to look at them? They weren't in the least bit feminine, but had a depth to them that I wouldn't normally associate with a man. There wasn't an ounce of fat anywhere on him from what I could see. I wouldn't go so far to say his looks were perfect, but I couldn't say that about most people. I wouldn't want him to be either. Imperfections make for a far more interesting person.

I hugged my arms around my middle and hoped I wasn't showing my muffin top.

"Why *did* you come here tonight?" There was no malice in those eyes. Gareth was curious, was taking the time to get to know me, even if it was only for one night. That was more than I could say about a lot of the men I'd been dating. Connie would, of course, argue that meant I was dating the wrong guys. I couldn't disagree with her.

Why did I come here tonight? It was more than pressure from Connie to get out and explore my options. It was probably the first time I took a chance on something like this, reached for something that I didn't simply want, but needed. This time I made sure to hold his gaze. I didn't want him to have any false impressions.

"Because I needed to know." And that was the God's honest truth. Saying I was curious was all well and good, but there was a lot more to it than that. I had to know if this was really who I was, or if it was nothing more than a fantasy. If it was the latter, then I would go home and buy up every e-book I could find with BDSM as the theme. If it was the former . . . well, I'd have to figure that out as I went.

He gave my knee a final squeeze before letting his hand dangle once more. "Then I'll help you."

My head began to spin and I had to pull in a few deep breaths to settle my nerves. I'm not sure if it was relief or fear, but either way it was a rush.

"This is really going to happen." Yes, I'd paid the money, but this whole night didn't seem real yet. A wonderful dream with the perfect man cast as my Dom. A bevy of undiscovered pleasures stretched out before me.

"If you want it to. But only if you're honest with me and yourself. I'm not a miracle worker, a psychologist, or a magician. We'll be in this together tonight, taking things as far as you want them to go. But only if you're honest with both of us."

I nodded. Yeah, I got that and for once the idea of laying it all out there for someone to see didn't freak me out. "I think I'm a submissive."

"And you wanted to spend some time with a Dom to find out for certain?"

"Yeah."

"Why the auction? I'm sure Connie could have put you in touch with some people if you had questions."

"She'd tried, but I always wussed out. She was the one who suggested I come tonight. I wanted something . . ."

"Safe?"

"Contained. If things weren't what I'd expected, I wanted to make sure it only lasted one night."

"Why?"

Licking my lips, I tried to find the right words. "If things didn't go the way I hoped they might, I knew I would be able to walk away. This is only for one night."

Master Gareth nodded. He linked his fingers together and leaned a bit farther forward on his feet. "Why?"

I twisted in my seat. "I've had a few boyfriends in the past, but I never really felt satisfied with them. I was drifting along and none of them seemed able to anchor me."

"Was there anything any of them did sexually that aroused you?"

Poor John. The memory of his face and the look he'd had on it when I'd asked him to spank me was forever burned there. "Spankings were good for me. None of them were willing to try anything more than that. I think I freaked a few of them out with even the suggestion of something more."

Master Gareth got to his feet but didn't move away. He towered over me, his groin just about at face level. The leather pants left little to the imagination, hugging his half-hard cock.

Oh my.

It would be so easy to lean forward and press my face against the hard ridge of his shaft. I would mouth at him until he pulled me away by my hair, yanked the button from its mooring, and shoved his cock in my mouth.

"What do you fantasize about when you are alone? When there's nothing but you and your handy vibrator, what do you think about?"

Yeah, I was blushing hard. Though if it was from the heated nature of my thoughts or the need to spell out what I did when I got myself off, I couldn't be sure. I imagined it would be poor form to say "you" given I'd just met the man. Honest, but unnecessary pressure. Maybe he wouldn't mind?

"I'm not sure I can put it into words." I licked my lips in an attempt to cover up the blatant lie. I didn't know if I would sound like a freak for saying the truth out loud.

"Liz, I want you to close your eyes." I did without hesitation. It was getting easier to do what he said. "Now, tell me what you see."

I squeezed my hands a bit tighter in my lap. The images that popped into my head were always consistent, always set to get me turned on. "I see a man who is larger than me. He tells me what to do, takes away my choices in the bedroom. I don't want to think or decide or have to ask. I want him to simply know what I want when I want it. Apparently, I need to be with a mind reader."

"Liz." There was a warning note in his voice. It was strange to have someone pick up on my deflection techniques so quickly after first meeting them.

"I want to do what he says. If he wants to fuck my ass or have me give him a blow job, then that's what I'll do." I opened my eyes then and looked at him. *Really* looked at him. Somehow I knew there was something special going on tonight. I had taken a step into becoming someone else. An evolution into someone I didn't yet know.

I'm not sure what he saw standing there, what insights he gained by seeing me sitting before him, but something on his face changed. He leaned back and for a moment I understood what it would feel like to be under a magnifying glass.

I wasn't about to let that intense look scare me off. I knew I wasn't able to hold anything back now that I'd finally started talking. "Does that make me some sort of anti-feminist? I mean, what kind of woman wants to give up that kind of control to a man?"

Master Gareth didn't speak right away. While I knew what I said was probably the least shocking thing he'd ever heard in his life as a Dom, it was still a big step for me. I hadn't even said all of that to Connie, and she was a sub and definitely someone who would understand. But she was confident in her ability to let go and let Stephen flog her senseless, tie her up and do what he wanted, or withhold her orgasm until she was nearly delirious from need. They'd worked out the playbook and knew the calls.

I was still figuring out what the game was.

It was like taking a giant leap backward and becoming an awkward teenager once more. Never knowing what to do or say, what made me a freak or what was simply me being different. I wasn't old, but you'd think at twenty-six I'd have some of this stuff figured out by now.

"It's been my experience that it takes a very strong person to admit to needing help." He moved around to stand behind me. I shivered when I felt him lean forward so his mouth was close to my ear. "How long have you had these longings?"

Forever. "A while now."

"You wanted tonight to see if this was something you could do?"

"I need to know that this isn't some kind of mistake. Before I get into another relationship and fuck that up, too, I have to have my head around what it is I need. Before I ask someone for something I can't really see through. I—" This really shouldn't have been so difficult. I tended to do things the hard way when it wasn't necessary.

On impulse, I slipped from the chair to my knees and stayed there. If I couldn't make the words say what I wanted, then I could do this. Every cell in my body felt like it was vibrating with lust and impatience.

There was a pause and then the sound of the chair being pushed aside. "I have rules."

Rules were good. I liked rules.

His hand was warm on my shoulder and surprisingly comforting considering I'd just met the man. I'd never been foolish enough to believe in love at first sight, but even I couldn't deny the connection between us. While trust needs to be earned in most cases, for tonight I was willing to nudge my caution to the side and go with the flow.

"I've already told you rule one, refer to me as Sir."

I nodded. "Yes, Sir."

"See, you're doing fine already. Second rule, if I do something you don't like, you need to tell me. You will say red if you want me to stop. Yellow and I'll slow things down."

Colors were nice and simple. "I can do that."

The hand on my shoulder gave me a squeeze.

"Sir! I can do that, Sir." Dummy.

"Good girl."

His other hand took up position on my free shoulder. For the first time since I'd entered the club I felt grounded. I loved the feeling of his hands on my skin, how it drew another shiver from deep inside and caused my blood to surge. I was flying blind, but it was certainly a rush.

"Liz, I need to know if there is anything that freaks you out. The dark? Loss of breath? Being yelled at?"

"Nothing, Sir." There was that one time I'd freaked out when I'd gone indoor rock climbing, but I doubt he was going to send me scurrying up a wall anytime soon.

"Pain threshold?"

"One of the boyfriends I asked to spank me? When he did, his hand ended up hurting before my ass did. Sir." John had dumped me a week later. Despite what Connie said, I knew that was the reason why. He wasn't able to meet my gaze for days after, like I'd turned into some sort of three-headed freak. Sure, I might be better off without him, but it had still hurt.

The bastard.

Another squeeze, this time a lot harder. "From this point on I want you to stop thinking, Liz. I'm in charge now. Your body belongs to me and I will do with it what I want. Do you understand?"

I couldn't resist looking up at him. "This is really going to happen?"

I'm not sure if it was because we weren't that far into the scene, or if I was suddenly speaking to the man behind the Dom. Either way, Master Gareth gave me a small smile.

Logically I knew he wasn't two separate people, but I swear in that moment I could see a lot more than the Dom mask he'd been wearing up to this point. Maybe a mask wasn't the right description and he was simply good at hiding his emotions from others. Either way, I could tell he was used to keeping a part of himself held back.

I knew because it was something I did too.

Maybe someone had hurt *him* at one point? Wouldn't that be ironic?

Master Gareth's slight smile melted from his lips. The spark was still present in his eyes, which served to keep me calm and focused on him.

"You paid your money. I'm here to do what you want, which is to take over. If you *don't* want this, we can do something else. I would hate for you to feel some sort of pressure to continue on because of the auction, what Connie said, or any other reason. I don't mind talking about the lifestyle if you want more information. Though I could point you to some good Web sites for that."

"No! Sir, I'm good. Please. I'm ready for this."

Master Gareth reached down and cupped my chin. His gentle pull stretched my head back not quite to the point of pain. I gasped and let my eyes slip closed. He didn't let go, didn't relent. His fingers dug into the sensitive skin of my throat and gently squeezed. It wasn't enough to cut off my oxygen, but the sudden possessive and controlling move had my cunt clenching at the prospect of an amazing fuck.

"You need to stop your mind from spinning." He squeezed a bit harder. "Don't think for a moment I can't tell when you've got something buzzing around in there."

It was hard to blank my mind, though I made a valiant attempt. Instead, I concentrated on the pull of his calloused fingers across my throat, the ache of my neck muscles as I held the awkward angle. I didn't dare move. I didn't want to. It felt amazing to have his hand holding me firmly, pressing me into the floor with the strength of his will. Fuck, it was quite the rush.

"You will do what I say when I say. There will be no hesitation. If you have a genuine problem with anything, remember to say either red or yellow. *No* won't stop me. *Stop* won't stop me. Begging and pleading won't get you what you want either."

"Sir." And in that moment I felt relief.

He understood.

Gareth wasn't humoring me or trying to simply fulfill the auction bid. In a matter of a few minutes he got me. It was weird and electrifying all wrapped into one overwhelming package of awareness.

I couldn't stop the moan from escaping when he released the pressure on my throat. How could I miss the contact already? Was I that pathetic that the least bit of attention turned me into a panting, needy whore? The ping on the end of my nose had me snap my eyes open.

Right. No thinking.

"There is more to being a good submissive than doing what you're told. It's important, but not the be-all and end-all." He moved once again and with my eyes closed it was challenging to track him. "Tonight we'll keep things simple."

Would there be other nights? Would I even want other nights? I couldn't help but think yes, given how strongly I was reacting to him. It would be very easy to lose myself in him. Now I understood what Connie had been trying to tell me for months.

Without realizing he'd gotten close, I gasped when his hand plunged into my corset, found my nipple, and squeezed tight. The pain jerked me back to the room and Gareth.

"I said no thinking, Liz." The slight smile that had played on his lips was gone now. I was surprised how different he looked, all hard angles and iron control. "If you can't listen to me on this simple thing, then this will not work out."

Oh no, no, no, no! "I'm sorry, Sir. I'll do better."

"Yes, you will. Part of the problem is your clothing. It's a distraction. Take them off, fold them, and place them by the door.

Wait.

What?

"You're not moving. Do it now, Liz, or else leave."

There was no room for negotiation in that tone. There was no softness in his gaze or body. Gareth stood there staring at me, arms crossed and legs spread shoulder width apart. If I had been thinking I would have freaked out. I hardly knew the man and he wanted me to get naked in front of him while he remained fully clothed. It was probably the most insane thing I'd ever been asked to do in my life.

I don't think I've ever moved so quickly before in my life. Sure my fingers shook as I pulled at the knot holding the front of my corset together, but I somehow managed to get it open. The damn thing proved harder to fold than I first figured it would be. I didn't want him to change his mind and kick me out because I'd moved too slow, so I folded the damn thing in half and jogged over to the door to place it on the floor.

If nothing else, I could go with the flow.

My jeans were easier to fold, but ended up being harder to remove. I wasn't wearing panties beneath and he would get an eyeful right away. I'm still not sure what had possessed me to skip putting on my intimates, but it had somehow seemed appropriate given where the auction was being held. Honestly, I didn't think anyone would be in a position to have noticed.

Too late for regrets.

I kicked off my heels as I undid the button. The denim pulled off easily and I had it folded and placed on the corset before I turned around to face Gareth once more. I could feel the blush heat my face and I hoped he didn't hold that against me.

My hands twitched at my side as Gareth's gaze slid down my body. God, I wanted nothing more than to cover myself then. I'd never been particularly good at making it to the gym on a regular basis, so there was a bit extra of me around my middle, ass, thighs . . . okay every-where. Most men didn't seem to mind, but I'd always been self-conscious about my weight.

"Very nice." His words penetrated into me and I shivered.

Naked is as naked does, I guess.

"I want you to put your shoes back on and come over here."

My ankles were protesting the return of the heels, but I wasn't about to argue with him. It gave me a few precious seconds to regis-ter what was happening. Gareth had moved to the wall where there was a ring secured quite high up. I knew it was a spot where people could be secured, but there didn't seem to be anything with which to bind me. Maybe that's part of the advanced class. If I was very lucky and very good, maybe someday I'd get to take part.

I joined him by the wall, pleased that my ankles didn't buckle as I crossed the room. Even in my shoes, Master Gareth was taller than me by a good four or five inches. Maybe he was trying to make sure I didn't feel too threatened by his size out of the gate. I would have told him that regardless of my submissive tendencies, I've always had a thing for big men. The bigger the better, in my book. He was built like a brick shithouse, exactly the type of man I gravitated toward.

When I finally met his gaze once more, I could see something different. I'm not sure if he was simply happy to have a new playmate, or if I was so new I had that cute-puppy-dog look about me. Probably the latter. Connie always teased me about that.

"Liz, I want you to lift your hands above your head and press your back to the wall. I want you to stay there and not move."

For once my mind stayed quiet as I did what he asked. The wall was cold and my nipples went instantly hard. They ached in that pleasant way and if he were to tweak them now, I would have been begging to get fucked.

Oh, shit, I didn't even know if sex was on the agenda. Wouldn't that be a letdown after getting naked and horny? Also a waste of a perfectly sexy man.

I wasn't sure if I was allowed to watch him or not, but when he moved away toward the cupboard I couldn't stop looking. What the hell did they have in there? My pussy felt swollen in anticipation. I hadn't been this turned on in years, so much so, I think I could actually have had an orgasm from penetration. Normally I had to rely on either oral or my hand to get off. But nope, the mere sight of Gareth in front of what I assumed was a toy cupboard was enough to have me coming.

God, I hope sex is on the table.

Or at least an orgasm.

CHAPTER 3

Master Gareth kept his back to me while he continued to rummage in the cupboard. My arms were aching and I found it hard to breathe, holding my arms up and still. It reminded me of that one time I had to get a scan of my lungs at the hospital. I had to lie on a bed with my arms stretched above my head for a solid twenty minutes. You'd think it would be easy, but after three minutes I was ready to beg the technician to stop.

Turned me into a whiny kid in no time. This was almost as bad.

Big-girl panties, Liz.

"You're thinking again."

Shit. "Sorry, Sir."

"I can see we'll have to work you into that tonight. I would hate to have to punish you for something so simple."

Punishment? That sounded promising. It could totally be a good thing. "No, Sir."

Damn, what the hell was he searching for in there? The door to Narnia?

I shifted where I stood and couldn't help my internal snark from yammering away—that is, until he turned back around. Any additional smart-ass remarks fled my mind when I saw the look of feral mischief in his eyes and the object of his infernal search in his hands. For half a second my arms slipped down to cover myself, but I managed to remember his order and lifted them back into place.

It didn't stop me from swallowing noisily and staring at what he held dangling from his outstretched finger.

Those looked an awful lot like nipple clamps.

"You said you had a high pain threshold. Let's test that."

Now, I've never considered myself a prude, but the sight of the silver chain and mini vice grips was enough to get me squirming. Damn, this was going to hurt, wasn't it?

"Hands, Liz."

I jerked my arms back into place. "Sorry, Sir."

"I can see that's going to be hard for you to hold that position on your own. Good thing I have something to assist."

I'd been so distracted by the nipple clamps, I'd completely missed the length of cord draped over his shoulder. I swallowed and did my best to keep my breathing under control. The last thing I wanted was for him to mistake my barely contained excitement for a panic attack.

Maybe I'd been staring at the rope for longer than I'd realized because Master Gareth held out the end of the rope, circling the tip with his thumb.

"Have you ever been tied up before, Liz?" God, he was almost playful in his tone. How could he switch from being as strict as a drill sergeant to a teasing schoolboy in the span of a heartbeat? More importantly, why was I responding to both as strongly as I was?

"No, Sir." I shook my head for emphasis. "Not that it's a problem for me." Wouldn't want him to get the wrong impression.

Master Gareth came up to my side, standing only a few inches away. It was close enough to feel his body heat, but far enough away that I couldn't accidentally bump into him. This time he didn't say anything, but I knew what he was intending to do even before he moved. I'd heard the expression telegraphing one's movements before, but now I understood. It was fascinating to watch him move.

His hand was strong around my wrists, and his fingers dug into my flesh as he pulled my arms down in front of me. He held them still for a moment and the silent look he gave me was enough of a command not to move. The rope was smooth, silky even, as it slid across my skin. A riot of goose bumps exploded across my skin, making it even more sensitive than before.

I'd been a Girl Scout as a kid and had been one of the few in my troop to have passed the knot badge. Those looked to be quick release, which made the whole thing a little easier to get my head around. And while Connie trusted him, she wasn't here getting strung up by a man who would look perfectly at home on the cover of *GQ*.

I should have been freaking out. Wouldn't most people? But Master Gareth also left a length of the rope dangling enough that I would be able to free myself. When he finished, I tested them and found I could barely move my hands. The bindings were tight enough to stop me from moving, but not enough that I'd lose circulation.

And in a pinch I could get myself free from the rope. There is something exhilarating and terrifying about giving up total control to another person.

If I hadn't been half-delirious from the pleasure at finally getting closer to understanding the feelings that had been building in me for years, I wouldn't have been so startled when he tied the other end of the rope to the O-ring on the wall. What else was I expecting him to do with it? Lead me around the club like a dog?

Actually . . .

I gave another tug once he was finished securing the rope. There was no way I was going to be going anywhere. I had enough slack that I could easily move half a foot from the wall, but that was about it. Master Gareth could spin me around until I was dizzy, but I couldn't escape him.

Not that I wanted to.

So not going anywhere.

"Now, for the next part." The grin he gave me that time was positively satanic. If he'd sprouted horns then I wouldn't have been the least bit surprised. He held the nipple clamps so they touched my nose, forcing me to go cross-eyed so I could get a good look at them. "I can tell by your reaction you've never done this before."

I shook my head. "No, Sir. But I'm willing to try."

God, he had nice teeth. They were all I could watch as he lowered his mouth so that he hovered just above my nipple. No, he wouldn't actually—

"Fuck!" I bucked my hips and strained against the rope that held me in place as his lips wrapped around my nipple.

Hot, wet heat enveloped the hard tip and it was like a charge had been set in me. His wicked tongue tormented my peak until I felt his saliva cover a generous portion of my breast. With each flick of his tongue my cunt vibrated. I swear to God I could feel his tongue on my clit even though he was nowhere near it.

"God, yes."

In a beat his tongue was replaced with his teeth. I sucked in a lungful of air as the sharp bite chased the pleasure with pain. Except I wasn't pulling away from him—I wanted more. Master Gareth didn't stop, alternating between hard sucks and sharp nips. Connie had tried to explain to me once what it was like to experience this weird mix of pleasure and pain, the overwhelming presences she felt when the two collided inside her, and couldn't find the words.

I now understood why.

How can a person qualify heaven?

Then he stopped. Gareth lifted his head and covered my breast with his hand. "What was rule one?" He was squeezing hard, and shit that really did hurt.

My head became too heavy for me to hold and I let it fall forward. The air I managed to suck in gave me a chance to get my head back in the game.

Rule one? I shook my head, but he only squeezed more.

Rules. Right.

They were important and if I couldn't remember them he'd stop.

Stopping was bad.

"I have to call you Sir."

But he didn't relent with his touch. "Have you?"

Did I? Oh, shit. "No, Sir. I . . . I forgot."

There really wasn't any warning when he clipped the clamp on the dry nipple. I did cry out then as the pain spiked through my chest. It was so tight it felt like the skin was being burned by acid or eaten by ants. I don't remember feeling that type of pain before. Strange, though, the longer it burned the less I minded.

It was fascinating.

"What was the second rule, Liz?"

Huh?

I lifted my head so I could force my gaze from the clamped nipple to his eyes. Was he actually serious? Yes, of course he was. I sucked in a breath, but the motion caused my breast to move and the clamp to be jostled. Of course he was *serious*. Master Gareth didn't seem the type to fool around with his words or his actions. Everything he did in his life had a specific purpose.

"Liz, answer me or this ends now."

Second rule, second . . .

"I won't let things go too far if I can't handle it."

"What do you say to stop things?"

"Red to stop you, yellow to slow down. Begging will only make things worse."

He chuckled at that. "Not exactly, but correct on the important part."

With the dry palm of his hand Gareth wiped off the saliva from the nipple that had been lucky enough to enjoy his mouth. I knew what was coming, but bracing for the pain of the second clamp did nothing to dull the sensation. The skin was already super-sensitive from his pleasurable abuse. The clamp intensified things to a level I could barely comprehend.

"Take a deep breath, Liz."

I did without question. The blackness around my vision that I hadn't realized was even there began to recede. My head cleared enough that his facial features snapped into focus.

He was smiling at me now. Not a grin, not even with his lips. The smile shone out from his eyes and in that moment he was the most beautiful man in the world.

"Take another deep breath."

I did it again.

My body felt electric, my skin a giant receptor for every puff of air that swirled around the room. My cunt was soaked as I let myself sink into the pain, the pleasure. He owned my body now and I loved it.

The chain dangled between my breasts and pulled my nipples even as they bound me together. The pain hadn't dulled so much as transformed into something I wasn't fully able to wrap my head around. My gaze had fallen once more to where the clamps squeezed my sensitive flesh between the black rubber ends. The skin was beet red and distended into an odd shape. The contrast of the black and silver of the chain was mesmerizing.

Master Gareth hadn't moved since clamping me. I'm not sure if he was waiting for me to say red or something, but I wasn't about to. It felt too good to stop.

I was never going to stop.

When I met his gaze, I could tell he was checking to see if I was too out of it to continue. I'm not sure how he would be able to tell if I was. Maybe it's like a parent can always tell that their child is about to do something stupid when the house is too quiet.

I licked my lips but didn't quite have the energy to smile. I wasn't sure it was totally appropriate at any rate.

"Please, Sir. I-I can take more. I-I-I need to try. To see." Yeah, I remembered that he said begging wasn't likely to get me what I wanted; but hell, he needed to know that I was still on board with the program. If nothing else, I hoped it would prove that I was very pleased with my purchase and wanted to take things to the next level.

Because while getting tied up and clamped was pretty fucking great, I was more than aware there were far better things we could be doing here.

Despite his earlier words, Master Gareth did reach out and cup my cheek. His caress was gentle, reassuring, and confusing. I wasn't expecting a man as large as him, let alone a Dom, to touch me like that. Something flashed across his face, but it went too fast, and quite frankly I was too out of it to clue in to what it could possibly mean.

Whatever it was, the mood shifted when he stepped back and straightened to his full height. "Liz, I want you to turn around and face the wall. Don't move once you're in position."

Hell yeah.

It wasn't a big move, but for some reason my head spun along with my body. I tried to take a deep breath like he'd prompted earlier and pulled in a bit of extra air, but that sent another burst of lovely pain through my nipples. My pussy was still swollen and I could feel my wetness starting to cover my inner thighs. If I didn't get to come soon I was going to explode.

And not in the good way.

"Now that is a beautiful ass."

I groaned when his hands cupped my cheeks and gave my ass a good, hard squeeze. Master Gareth pulled at the flesh, exposing my hole to him. God, I was blushing again. I dropped my head forward and closed my eyes. How the hell could he look at me like that?

"Of course it's beautiful, Liz. You're a healthy woman who clearly looks after herself."

I jerked my head up then and tried to look at him from over my shoulder. How the hell . . . ?

He chuckled once more and I knew I was growing addicted to the sound of that low rumble of amusement. "I've been around enough naked women to know that the first time you all think the same thing. You've got too much around the middle. Your thighs are too big, ass too wide, cellulite. Why would a man want to see you with the lights on?"

Whoa.

"But you forget most men find your bodies beautiful no matter the shape. Your curves and bumps, the things you see as imperfections mark you as unique. We want to learn every inch of you, memorize what makes you moan and sigh."

As he spoke, Master Gareth slid his hand down the length of my leg, teasing the back of my knee, and cupped my calf. I shivered when he reached my ankle. Anything from that point down was basically a giant erogenous zone for me. He must have picked up on it and gave me a slight squeeze. "See. This is as much a turn-on for me as seeing your pussy."

Another gentle brush of his fingers along the edge of my ankle bone had me moaning. I pulled against my bindings and bucked my hips forward.

"Soon." He scraped the skin lightly with his nails.

I felt him stand up. What I wasn't expecting was the sharp slap of his hand against my ass. The left cheek flared up with pain that sent me staggering toward the wall. I gasped and widened my stance. I wasn't going to get caught off guard twice.

And yet, I totally was. Instead of another smack, he bracketed my hips with his hands and pulled me back.

"I want you to stick your ass out, but lean forward. That's it. Bow your back like a dog stretching. Good girl."

I let him maneuver me into the position he wanted. If I'd thought I'd been exposed earlier, then I was clearly an inexperienced fool. Standing like this, I was completely at his mercy, my ass being offered up as some sort of naughty sacrifice for him. Any fears I'd had about being naked in front of him were now gone. All I could focus on was the anticipation of getting a spanking, the type I'd fantasized about but had never asked for.

"I want you to stay exactly like that, Liz. Don't you move. Widen your legs a bit more. There you go. Now, I'm not going to spank you."

"What? No, Sir, please—"

"Not with my hand at least."

Oh. Oh, thank God.

It was so tempting to turn around to see what he was up to back there. But that would mean getting out of the position he'd put me into. I didn't dare.

Something cold touched both my ass cheeks when he finally returned. I couldn't tell what it was, but I leaned into it.

"I'm going to start you off with a little paddling. Think you will like that, Liz?"

"Yes, Sir. Please, I'd like to try that, Sir." I didn't even realize I was nodding until my head spun once more. Stopping, I let the tremor of excitement race through my body, making my arms and legs tingle and my chest tighten. I couldn't remember wanting something so much in my entire life.

Another squeeze, this time to my hip. "We're going to start simple. This is your first time doing anything like this and I don't want to push you too far."

A part of me wanted to reassure him that I was fully onboard with anything he had in mind—go to town, Sir, and spank me like there's no tomorrow—but the words dissolved in a moan when the paddle hit my ass. It didn't really hurt, more of a warm-up tap. Master Gareth followed it up with a second, then a third.

The skin was starting to heat up and I could feel a thin layer of sweat break out across me. I didn't understand why I was getting hot. I wasn't actually doing anything. But there I was, doing my best to ignore the errant trickles of sweat rolling down my neck and between my breasts. It irritated and excited me all at once.

"Time to play." I'm not sure if he was saying the words to me or to himself. Regardless, I tightened my thighs and got ready for what was to come.

This time when the wide, flat face of the paddle hit my left ass cheek I knew he wasn't holding back. The flash of pain across my ass had me crying out. But unlike before, Master Gareth gave me no time to recover. Three smacks in rapid succession and all in different locations had my skin flaring with heat.

It felt so good, I didn't even question it.

"Two more and then we're going to switch to something new."

"Shit." Damn, I didn't mean to actually say that out loud. "Sir." No sense in inviting trouble when I didn't want any.

He didn't laugh that time, but I could feel his smile without even seeing it. My skin tingled with awareness and a pleasant flutter bounced around my insides.

The final two slaps were one to each butt cheek and he used his hand rather than the paddle. My pussy twitched again at the connection of flesh on flesh. I wanted his hands all over my body, touching and pulling at every bit of me. Those two quick hits weren't going to be enough to satisfy me. The bastard was the most addictive drug in the universe and I wanted to OD on him.

Unfortunately for me, more of Master Gareth was going to have to wait a bit.

The long leather tendrils of a flogger tickled my shoulder and spilled down the front of my chest. The gentle caress was in stark contrast to the throb of my nipples and the burning of my ass.

"I think you'll like this." Master Gareth ran the flogger along the back of my shoulder blades. The leather was soft and pulled up another riot of goose bumps from my skin. I felt like every inch of me was on fire and there was nothing that would soothe the burn. "It's not going to be exactly what you're expecting, though."

At this stage I couldn't think further than the next sensation. It was becoming increasingly difficult to form thoughts, and talking was apparently something I wasn't really able to do anymore. I knew I had to keep my head. It would be too easy to slip along on this strange haze of pleasure and pain that ebbed and flowed within me now.

Master Gareth started easy with the flogger. The steady back and forth, the leather slapping at about my shoulder blade to trickle down diagonally to my hip, took away my ability to think completely. It was soothing, like a really awesome massage or thorough backrub. The world slipped away at that point. I wasn't conscious of the club, Connie and what she was doing, the extra ten pounds I'd been carrying around for a while now. Everything faded away.

It was just me and Master Gareth. He was leading me down a path and I was more than happy to follow.

CHAPTER 4

The slap of leather tendrils against my skin had changed. They were connecting harder and faster than before, but he'd increased the intensity so slowly I hadn't noticed. I'm not even certain he realized he'd changed what he'd been doing. Now instead of the lulling caress, the leather nipped at me, prickling the skin like pins and needles.

Time no longer held any meaning. If you'd asked me how long I'd been like this, trussed up and begging, I wouldn't have been able to even guess. But the pain in my arms was starting to move from being a turn-on to downright painful. It wouldn't have stopped me from wanting to stretch out and beg him to fuck me, but it might have made things challenging.

Please God, let him fuck me soon.

The tempo of the flogging changed again. He must have realized I'd started thinking again and wanted to jerk me back to what was important. It amazed me how he was able to do that, be so in tune with me and my thoughts—probably more so than I was even aware. Master Gareth increased the intensity once more. Each blow sent me jerking forward, pulling on my shoulders. God, that was really starting to hurt now. But I didn't want to stop him. Not before I got everything I'd wanted from tonight. Everything I needed.

Everything I might be too scared to ask for again.

I would have said something, yellow maybe to give myself a

break, when Master Gareth suddenly stopped and tossed the flogger to the floor. He moved to stand in front of me, ducking at an awkward angle so he could get his head beneath my outstretched arms.

I opened my mouth to speak, but nothing came out. I couldn't even moan when he cupped my cheek once more and rubbed his thumb across the sensitive skin below my eye. My body didn't know how to register the gentleness in his touch. I wasn't so much numb to it, but it took me awhile to realize what the feeling was.

"You need to stop?"

Licking my lips, I managed to whisper a soft, "No."

"You're crying, Liz. Is the pain too much? I need you to tell me."

Crying? I wasn't, was I? "No, Sir."

Master Gareth frowned. I didn't like to see him looking like that, concerned for me, and know that it was my fault. There was something about him . . . it was wrong to see him so worried when he was taking such good care of me. I wanted to make him happy. *Needed* to thank him for everything he'd done for me so far. Right then, he was the most important man in the world.

And where the hell was that coming from?

"Please, Sir. I-I need to. I mean, I want to—"

He moved his hand from my cheek and slid it down the side of my throat. He pressed against my windpipe in the same fashion he'd done when we'd first started. This time, I saw black spots within seconds and my head swam. I could still breathe, but only shallowly.

Surprisingly, I wasn't worried at all about my safety. Connie had vouched for him and I'd learned a surprising amount about him in the short time we'd been together in here. He'd taken the time to stop and check, make sure I was okay and that everything wasn't becoming too much. Those weren't the actions of a man who'd intentionally hurt a woman.

It gave me the freedom to close my eyes and focus my concentration on how fast my heart was pounding, how the moment his hand released the pressure on my throat I sucked in a deep breath and was rewarded with a rush of adrenaline through my body.

Master Gareth's hand continued its journey down my body, pausing to offer homage to the clamps that still adorned my nipples. Tugging lightly on the chain, his gaze shifted from one red tip to the other. He brushed his thumb across the end, but I couldn't feel the touch.

"Time to take these off." He moved his head so his mouth was only an inch away, his hot breath rolling over my sweat-covered skin. "This is going to hurt."

Given everything else he'd done to me tonight, I really wasn't expecting the pain to be anything I couldn't handle.

What a fucking idiot I was.

The second he released the clamp and the blood rushed back to where it was supposed to be, pain lanced through my breast and into my chest. It was near blinding to me in intensity until the heat from his mouth covered the abused tip.

The flicking of his tongue across my nipple wasn't enough to begin with. I was numb to the pleasure for a few moments until the sensitivity of the skin changed and I could once more register the amazing pressure of him suckling me. I leaned forward as far as I could, wanting to shove as much of my breast into his mouth as possible. I managed only a few inches when his strong arm came around my waist and held me still.

No, no, no, no, I needed more.

I was a little better prepared for the removal of the second clamp, but only just. Again, I waited for the comfort his mouth brought me, moaning and begging him to bring an end to my suffering. The grip around my waist tightened and I could feel his fingers fan out to cover most of my lower back.

That touch, those few points of contact, grounded me back to earth. In my head, I imagined my skin was stretched to the point of splitting. Something new and wonderful would burst through and Liz wouldn't exist. I'd be a new, amazing creature, one worthy of being with Master Gareth.

Like the crying, I honestly wasn't even aware of my pleas until he lifted his head and pressed a kiss to the center of my forehead. "Shh, it's all going to be fine, Liz."

I sniffed. I didn't want to think about the state of my face. "Please." I no longer knew what I was asking for.

"You've been a good girl. Listening to everything I've asked you to do. You've done much better than the few first-timers I've been with." He slid his hand around and cupped the back of my neck. "Hell, you've done better than some of the more experienced subs I've played with."

It was then that it hit me. I know it's a cliché to say, but it really did feel like an electric current raced through my body as the thought flashed through my mind.

I wasn't going to be able to do this with anyone else.

Why I thought that, I wasn't certain. I'd just met the man. It certainly wasn't love that I was feeling. This was something else, and for the life of me I couldn't put my finger on what it was. But I knew as certain as my name was Liz Marie Coghlan that I wouldn't be able to accept anyone but Master Gareth as a Dom.

"Do you want to come?"

My head fell forward and my eyes widened. "Sir?"

"Do. You. Want. To. Come?" Each word was punctuated with a small bite across my breast. "You can, if you want. But you need to do something first. A test, if you will."

Tests? Now? I could barely think, let alone do basic math. "If I have to, Sir."

"I'm going to take your hands down first. I want you on your knees."

Those few words were magic to my ears, though *on your knees* trumped *take your hands down,* surprising given how much they hurt. Unfortunately, that gave my brain enough room to kick in. I couldn't take in much air and the pleasant dizziness of my head was quickly becoming something more alarming.

"My arms . . . fast, Sir." I sucked in a breath. "Getting hard to breathe."

I can honestly say that I haven't seen someone move that quickly before. It took only one sharp yank and Master Gareth had the rope free from the hook on the wall. But instead of letting my arms fall down, he draped them over his shoulder while he helped me to the floor. Apparently, my legs were no longer working either. Strange, given I'd been standing fine up to then.

He carefully supported the weight of my arms, shifting me around once I was down so my hands were now resting in my lap. When he started massaging my shoulders with his free hand, I groaned.

Christ, that felt good.

Despite the physical exertion I'd been put through over the past . . . God only knew how long, I didn't feel the least bit sleepy. I was well aware of the throbbing of my cunt and the need to have something, anything shoved into it. Before I realized what I was doing, I started to squirm. The press of my super-charged clit between my thighs was nearly enough to set me off.

"Don't you dare."

He said the words softly, but there was no mistaking the steel behind them. With a slight shift, he moved my thighs apart, removing both the sensation and the temptation of being able to grind myself into blissful orgasm.

"And don't pout."

"I never pout. Sir."

Master Gareth chuckled once more. Yup, I really loved the sound of that. "Next time I'll have to take a picture. If that's not a pout, then I need a new definition." He flicked my bottom lip with his finger for good measure.

"Are you ready for my little test, Liz?"

No. "Yes, Sir."

He got to his feet and took a few steps back. The change in angle forced me to look up at him. It was the first time I'd been able to see all of him since he'd walked over to me with the clamps dangling from his fingertip.

His T-shirt now held dark patches of sweat, making the cotton cling to him even tighter than before. I'd never stopped to consider how difficult it would have been for him to wield the paddle and flogger. God, I wasn't even certain how long he'd been going at it.

The next thing my gaze landed on was the very impressive bulge pressing against the front of his leather pants. Damned impressive.

"Liz, look at me."

I cocked an eyebrow. "I am, Sir."

"My eyes, if you please."

Oh, oops. When I finally looked into those rich brown eyes, I saw that he was laughing at me again. There was even an accompanying twitch of his lips.

"What was the first rule?"

"To always call you Sir, Sir."

The response had been so automatic I hadn't even thought about it. Knowing that I'd made it a part of me already was thrilling.

Master Gareth approved, too, if his growing smirk was anything to go by. "And the second?"

"I need to say yellow to slow you down and red to stop you. You also said that begging wouldn't get me what I wanted, but I'm willing to try now, Sir. Please, Master Gareth, I-I-I need." Shit. I closed my eyes, took a breath, and forced my concentration. "I need to taste you. P-p-please c-can I suck you, Sir? Please, *please.*"

"This isn't supposed to be about sex." His frown deepened as he laced his hands behind his back. For a moment, images of military officers and errant enlisted women popped into my brain. "You bought my services as a Dom."

"Please." Now I knew I was crying. "I know it's not, Sir. I know. But I wanted to thank you for, for everything."

The words dried up then. I knew if he wasn't going to grant me this favor, there'd be nothing I could do to change his mind. He wasn't a prostitute and I certainly wasn't a whore. I wouldn't force him, even if I could. The trust I'd shown him had to go both ways. If he didn't want me . . .

I don't know what I'd do.

"Liz." He turned his head and licked his lips. "Shit."

I didn't move. We were both walking on the edge of something very sharp. One misstep and not only would we fall, we'd be shredded as we went down.

"Liz." He tried again. Some of the confidence had come back into his voice. "These scenes can be very intense. Your first time, in many ways, is like being a virgin all over again. It will set the stage for all of your other encounters. I don't want you feeling that sex has to be the culminating event. There are other options."

God, even self-confident men could be stupid at times. "I know that, Sir."

For a moment I thought he would give in.

"Lay back on the floor. Spread your legs wide."

I moved quickly, ignoring the way every nerve in my body seemed to quiver. I knew my inner thighs were glistening with my juices. I didn't think I could ever remember being this turned on.

"Wider, Liz."

The stretch in my muscles felt good, especially after having been on my feet in these awful heels for so long. Even better was Master Gareth's hands on my foot, rubbing small circles along the top.

"Next part of the test, Liz. Don't move."

I closed my eyes, mostly because it gave me deeper enjoyment of the feeling of his fingers against my skin. My nipples throbbed in contrast to the butterfly touches and soft scrapes of his nails across my toes.

He slowly made a path up my body. The longer he took the harder it was to hold my body in check. I needed to move, to squirm, wiggle my way closer to his fingers, his hands, him.

It felt as if every cell in my body was vibrating, trying to explode or implode, or something. The pleasure his fingers elicited became like metal in my blood, scraping along the inside of my skin, following his touch.

"God, you're so wet." Master Gareth slid the palm of his hand along the inside of my thigh. "I bet I could make you come just by talking to you."

Normally I'd have a smart-ass remark for him, but my brain had gone on vacation with no sign of its return. My body had been reduced to a quivering mess beneath his touch.

"I . . . God, Liz."

Opening my eyes, I moaned at the sight of him. Master Gareth had pulled his T-shirt off, leaving himself beautifully bare-chested. His skin had a light dusting of dark hair that curled around his nipples and led down to his crotch. I would have given anything in that moment for him to strip off the rest of his clothing. I wanted to feel the press of his body hard against mine while he fucked me here on the floor.

I bit down on my bottom lip, using the pain to focus my mind. "Please."

What I wasn't expecting was the slight shake of his head and for him to run his hand down his face. "Shit."

"Please." *Oh, God, don't leave me like this, not when I'm finally so close to what I need.*

There was something else going on with him, even in my lust-addled state I could tell. I knew he wanted nothing more than to fuck me, the hard outline of his cock told me that much.

"Master Gareth?"

I'm not sure what decision he'd come to, but he cut the air with his hand. "Close your eyes. I told you not to move."

He didn't give me much time to react before he maneuvered his way between my thighs, lifting my legs to drape over his shoulders. I registered his hot breath on my pussy half a second before his tongue lapped at my clit.

I screamed.

The touch was so gentle and yet he could have hooked me up to an electric motor for all the power that was in that soft slide of wet flesh on flesh. The throbbing in my nipples intensified as the blood raced even faster through me.

Two fingers pushed into my cunt, spreading me open as he began to pump his hand in time with his licks. The tips of his fingers pressed against the top of my pussy, dragging another moan from me. Then he switched the slow, easy rhythm into something harder, faster.

Master Gareth latched on to my clit with a suction that rivaled anything I'd ever felt before. As he fucked me with his fingers, he dipped his free hand down to play with my asshole. Oh, Christ, I'd never let anyone touch me there before.

He didn't wait or ask permission. Using the copious amounts of my juices, he slicked up his other fingers and pressed one into my ass.

God, I'd never felt so full. So possessed. So utterly owned.

All thoughts of orders, rules, and tests evaporated then. My hands flew to his head and I squeezed his hair. I was so damn close to release, to finally getting what I needed, I would never let him—

Master Gareth sucked hard and pressed his fingers in deep simultaneously, and that was it for me.

My orgasm was like a brush fire, igniting every nerve in my body like a cascade. Every muscle tensed until my back arched off the floor and I pressed my hands hard against his head. He groaned and doubled his efforts on my clit, sucking and teasing until my body had nothing left to give.

I'm pretty sure I passed out then, because the next thing I remember was turning my head to the side and burying my nose in Master Gareth's T-shirt. I'm not sure when he'd put it under my head, but the thin cushion was a welcome relief from the cold.

"You with me again?"

I had enough energy in me to lift my head off the floor and see him sitting on the chair where we'd started our evening's adventure. I flopped back to my makeshift pillow, unfortunately connecting a bit too hard, and sent my vision swimming.

"I think so."

"Here, drink this." He was crouched down beside me in a moment, a sports drink held between us. "You'll want to have Connie or someone drive you home. You'll find your reactions might be a bit slow until you get a good night's sleep."

Now, I may have just had the most mind-blowing orgasm of my

life and my brain was still a bit scrambled, but I could tell there was something not quite right.

"You didn't come." It didn't take a rocket scientist to figure that one out.

He held my gaze to the point of it being uncomfortable. But before I felt obligated to look somewhere else, he dropped his gaze to the floor.

"You know, you're a beautiful woman, Liz."

Ah shit.

"Tonight was pretty damn amazing."

Somehow I found the strength to hold up my hand. I never considered myself an idiot, and could hear the ginormous *but* coming my way. I couldn't handle it. God, I'd just started to figure this shit out, I couldn't handle . . . I mean, I knew who I was now . . . I was a sub and he was . . . he was *it!*

"Please don't." Somehow my voice wasn't too shaky. I licked my dry lips and chanced another sip of the drink. "You don't have to say it."

"I think I need to." He brushed my bangs from my face. "You are beautiful, you know."

Turning onto my side, I made sure my back was to him. My nose was fully pressed into his shirt now and Goddammit why couldn't I ever get this shit to fall in my favor. Just once would be nice.

"If I said it wasn't about you, I know you wouldn't believe me." His fingers now brushed the back of my neck. "You're on the beginning of this journey, Liz. You need to find the right person."

"You could be the right one." Yes, that sounded childish, but what the hell did it matter anyway. He was getting out of my life as quickly as he'd fallen in.

"Or I could be severely fucked up. You don't know me, Liz."

Master Gareth moved away then, and I knew this was my last chance to see him. I rolled onto my opposite side and watched him pick up the items we'd used and put them in a special bin by the door.

"I still have your shirt." My fingers were bunched around the fabric, my knuckles white.

"Keep it. You might want to cover up."

"What about you?"

I hated the idea of him going back out into the club where others would be able to see the beauty of his sculpted muscles, his hard angles, and the tension that now ran through his body. Because one look from anyone out there and they would know that Master Gareth was leaving this room in a swath of sexual frustration.

He turned to look at me once the room was tidied. "I have my jacket behind the stage. Christian was keeping an eye on it."

"Oh."

"Take your time getting up and dressed. No one will come in here until they know you've gone."

"So, that's it?" The hollowness that always crept into my chest after it was clear one of my boyfriends was leaving me was back.

Which in itself was bizarre because we'd just met. There'd been no commitments, or words of love; hell, he hadn't even fucked me yet. There was no reason why Master Gareth opening the door should feel as if my heart were being torn out of my chest. He owed me nothing.

But he didn't walk through the door immediately. Master Gareth pressed his forehead to the doorjamb, closed his eyes, and chuckled. "Fuck."

I didn't say anything else. What else could I say? I'd bought him for one night, to teach me if I could be a submissive or not. That was it. And he more than lived up to his part of the deal.

"I . . . Liz, you're shiny and new. Some Dom out there is going to be very fortunate to have you. Please take care of yourself. Say hi to Connie for me."

Then he left, shutting the door with a soft click.

CHAPTER 5

While I've never been one for grand gestures or drama of any sort, the week after the charity auction I submerged myself deep in the well of my own personal pity party. I'd never felt so dismissed before, and I hated how it cut into my self-perception. Connie always said that what I lacked in experience I made up with enthusiasm. Feeling sorry for myself was apparently no exception.

The week after the charity auction dragged on to the point of pain. I went to work, chatted with Connie, went to the gym, and participated in all the things that made up my life. I smiled at work and moped at home, but all the while the wheels were slowly turning in my head.

I had to come up with a plan.

There was no reason why I had to continue on like some kind of sap. I was a twenty-six-year-old woman with a brain in my head. It was time for me to use it.

I was a sexual submissive. Okay, that was fine. I could deal with that.

I had two options on how to proceed with that knowledge. I could hop on to one of the sites Connie recommended or join the club and make a few inquiries. I could go on the hunt for the perfect Dom, someone who would be willing to take me to the places I needed to go. Maybe, if I was lucky, I might even find someone who would want more than that, an actual relationship.

Or I could track down Master Gareth and find out what the hell was going on with him.

Because the more I thought about that night, the more I realized that there was something, some spark between us. I wasn't ready to walk away from that. Not without a fight. So, fuck him and his noble gestures, I wanted an explanation.

I came to my decision on Thursday. Normally, nothing exciting ever happens on a Thursday, but like everything else in my life, I apparently was going to change that as well.

"Connie?"

"Yo." She was in the kitchen, putting her glass dildo in the dishwasher.

Christ. "Con, I thought I asked you not to do that anymore?"

"You said with dishes in there! It's empty."

Once again I had to applaud my self-restraint when it came to dealing with my best friend and roommate. "You and Stephen know the Dom from the auction, right?"

"Gareth?" Connie shut the dishwasher and flicked it on before I could protest further. "Yeah, he plays rugby with Steve on Sundays. He's a prof in the English department at the university."

Fleeting memories of Master Gareth's introduction came back to me. "So, he's smart."

"And currently single." Connie rested her hip against the now-shuddering dishwasher. "His wife died in a car accident four years ago. Steve said it nearly destroyed Gareth. She was his sub as well as his wife. He's only started getting back into the scene this past year, though he hasn't done very much."

The knot of tension that had taken up residence in my chest since he'd walked away from me pulled tighter before it finally started to slip. "That's horrible." I crossed my arms, trying to fight off the chill I suddenly felt. "You said you and Stephen did a scene with him."

"Yup, totally hot, too. Steve was trying to help him get back into things. It was one of the reasons we wanted you to buy him. We both figured you'd be perfect for each other."

So, it really wasn't just me who'd been set up that night. "That's why you and Stephen gave me the money."

Connie shrugged. "We wanted to make sure both of our favorite peeps are going to be okay when the two of us go off and get married."

Whoa. "What?" I think my voice went up three octaves. "Congratulations!"

There was hugging and laughter and questions then. I might be a tad neurotic, but I pride myself on being a good friend. "Have you set a date?"

"Not yet. Probably next spring. I need to sit down and plan everything out. Need to know how many people I plan to invite. How many plus ones to plan for."

Subtle Connie.

The sigh that escaped me was pretty much the most pathetic sound I'd ever made. "He made it pretty clear he wasn't interested."

"He's a man. Just because he's a Dom doesn't mean he can't be an idiot about his personal life."

"Yeah, but—"

Connie slapped my arm. The bitch. "No *yeah buts*. He's teaching a night class tonight. Go talk to him."

Which is how I found myself leaning against the cold, beige-colored cinderblock wall of the university's basement hallway, waiting for Gareth's nineteenth-century literature class to end.

Being a business major, I never got into the whole love of stories thing, but there was something engaging about listening to Master Gareth—well, Professor Baxter, or I guess I should start thinking of him as simply Gareth—go on about the themes of family and power in whatever book they'd been discussing.

The class was dismissed with a clap of his hands and a cheer. "Okay, be prepared to discuss George Eliot and *Silas Marner*. Yes, you have to read the book. The movie doesn't count. Yes, I can tell the difference."

A few of the students eyed me as they shuffled past and out into the night. I doubt any of them had a clue what their professor got up to after hours. I know I would have been shocked as all get out to learn one of my profs was into sexual domination. Mind you, most of my professors were stodgy business guys who didn't seem aware of anything beyond microeconomics. Clearly, I had chosen the wrong major.

Gareth was shutting down the AV system when I stepped into the lecture hall, the glow from the screen casting interesting patterns across his face. The students left the room surprisingly quickly, leaving us alone.

"Hi." My heart pounded in my chest and my hands were damp. I don't think I'd been more nervous about anything in my life, and that included the auction.

Gareth instantly froze. I wasn't sure if Connie or Stephen was going to give him a heads-up about my impending arrival, but clearly that hadn't happened. He let out a short huff and finished turning off the computer. But once the power had finished powering down, he didn't move away from the podium.

Shit, this wasn't supposed to be how things went.

I moved a bit farther into the hall, casting a quick glance around to ensure we were in fact on our own. "I only ever took Introduction to Literature back in my first year. Is *Silas Marner* a good book?"

"It's about a man falsely accused of theft. He finds a child and raises her as his own. In the end his life is better for having taken her in."

"A little light reading then." I chuckled. The story actually sounded interesting. "I should pick it up."

"Why are you here, Liz?"

There was no malice in his words. Maybe a bit of frustration and a lot of confusion, but not anger. I took that as a good sign and crept a few steps closer.

"You wear glasses." They were the wire frame ones that I always found sexy on men. "You didn't have those on the other night."

"I wear contacts to the club." Gareth tightened his grip on the podium. "Liz?"

"I've been moping."

He cocked an eyebrow. "Moping?"

"According to Connie, yes. It's not something that I tend to do very often."

With a gentle tap against the side of the wood, Gareth stepped out from behind his barrier. "Why have you been moping?"

"I missed you."

See, my plan of attack was to try to be as honest with what I wanted from him as I could. In the past, my attempts to be subtle with the men in my life rarely panned out in my favor. And really, Gareth didn't seem the type to appreciate anything less than the total truth.

But when he sighed and pinched the bridge of his nose, I had the fleeting thought that my plan might be lacking. "We've only known each other one night."

Ah, but I'd been ready for that rebuttal. Sliding my ass onto the nearest desk, I crossed my legs. My choice of keeping on the skirt I'd worn to work was completely calculated. So was the lack of panties.

"Yes, but you have to admit the circumstances were far from normal." My nipples were still tender, especially when I tugged on them while I got myself off. I'd been doing that a lot since that night.

Gareth took a step closer, but the distance between us was still vast. "You don't know anything about me."

"I know. I'm not asking to go steady, just an opportunity to get to know you." And here was where things were going to get challenging. "I really think we might . . . you know . . . get along." I shrugged.

"You do." He took another step. "Or do you think no one else will be able to give you what you had the night of the auction? Because I can tell you right now that's not true. There are many men, some far better than myself, who can take you to the places you need to be."

Shit, maybe he really didn't want anything to do with me. I slipped to my feet but didn't move far from the desk. "I know that."

"Then there's no reason why you should feel obligated to chase after me."

"You think that's what this is? Obligation?"

"Liz, up until a week ago, you weren't even certain you were a submissive. I opened your eyes to a new world. It's not so unbelievable."

Was he right?

Stepping closer, I tried to force myself to really look at the man in front of me. There wasn't an inch of leather anywhere on his body. A pair of beige dress pants hugged his waist, and I could only imagine what his ass looked like encased in cotton. The button-down dress shirt was open at the neck, giving me a tantalizing glimpse of the toned body beneath. In many ways, he looked nothing like the Dom who'd worked me into a frenzy.

Then I looked into his eyes and there was no mistaking whom I was talking to. The vulnerability he'd tried to cover up, the few slips I'd only later realized I'd seen. If anything, Gareth was, in a strange way, laying himself out before me much as I'd done for him.

I took another step closer. "Connie said your wife passed away?"

He flinched. "Car accident. No one's fault, just slippery roads."

"She was your sub, right?" His hands were balled up at his sides, but he said nothing else. "You feel like you let her down. That you should have been able to do something to look after her, make things better?"

"Did Stephen tell you that?" Gareth didn't sound angry, more akin to exhausted.

"No, I guess it's pretty obvious that as someone who takes pride in looking after his lady you'd be killing yourself on the inside about this."

"Don't pretend to know me, Liz. I get the impression you don't really know yourself."

The barb hurt more than I was willing to let on. Instead, I decided to change tactics. Holding out my hand, I didn't bother to wait for him to take it before I began speaking.

"Hello. My name is Liz Coghlan. I'm twenty-six and work as a community outreach specialist with Schultz Associates. I got the job as part of their new grad program, but I've been moving up in responsibility."

He didn't move to take my hand. Gareth frowned, but his hands slowly started to relax by his sides.

"I've only had three serious sexual relationships over the years. The last one was John. He's the one I told you about who spanked me. I got dumped the week after we'd tried. He most definitely wasn't a top."

Gareth smirked.

"I'm not sure how serious a relationship I want right now. I work long hours and am still trying to figure out what all this means. I do want to find a man who might be willing to help me explore my submissive streak. And possibly go to the movies with me. I love horror films."

Gareth took a step closer. "Horror? Not romance?"

"Horror or action. With lots of explosions. Or those really bad B movies where even the actors know things are over the top."

My arm was starting to shake now from the strain of keeping it held out straight. I was going to have to let it drop soon if he didn't take it.

"I talk a lot, though not during movies because that's plain rude. I love pizza with olives, getting my ass spanked, and learning new things. Who wrote *Silas Marner* again?"

"George Eliot." Gareth reached out and took my hand. "Nice to meet you, Liz."

His fingers were warm as they wrapped around mine. The squeeze of our hands together sent an immediate shiver through my body. No, it wasn't just Gareth's control or raw sexuality. I knew instinctively that I'd like *him*.

"I haven't done this in a while." He stepped a bit closer but didn't let go of his hold on me. "I'm not an easy person to get to know."

"That's fine. I'm not asking to go steady."

"But you are asking for a relationship."

Connie was right, he really could be an idiot. "I'm asking for a chance to get to know you. I might discover you're a jerk and want nothing more to do with you."

Gareth snorted and then started like the noise surprised him. "I can be. An overbearing one if my late wife was to be believed."

Giving him a squeeze, I turned his hand over and cradled it in my palms. "I have an idea."

"You don't give up easily, do you?"

"Nope." I smiled and for the first time that night began to relax. "Do you want to hear it?"

"Fine."

"Why don't we go for a coffee at the little shop here on campus? I remember they make decent banana bread. You can tell me a few things about your wife, how you met her and stuff. I'll tell you about my first year rooming with Connie and how that insanity happened. Then if things go smoothly, we can see about another coffee on another day. Sound good?"

Gareth took a step back, breaking my contact with his hand. Before I could ask him what he was doing, he'd grabbed his attaché case and jacket. Instead of going to the door like I'd expected, he simply stood there. Damn, he was frowning again, which meant he was thinking. I was an expert on how easy and deadly overthinking things could be.

I couldn't have that. And he didn't deserve to continue to beat himself up over something he couldn't have controlled.

Slapping my hands against the side of my leg, I marched over to the door. I stopped before leaving, turned, and cocked an eyebrow. "I drink my coffee black."

Gareth's lips twitched and he shook his head. I crossed my arms and narrowed my gaze. "The banana bread sucks there now. They have a new owner."

"Then we'll buy muffins."

I took another step forward so I was standing on the threshold.

He smiled, nodded once, and followed me through the door.

PART 2

TRAINING THE DOM

CHAPTER 6

You know, life seems a lot less complicated when you're naked on the floor and your hands are tied behind your back. I mean, it's hard to worry about bills, project reports, or that annoying, pain-in-the-ass, bitch-faced coworker when you are getting flogged and there isn't anything you can do about it.

Not that I'd want to.

Fuck that.

Master Gareth was somewhere behind me being extremely quiet. I'm always amazed at how he's able to do that—be still and calm. I have so much energy inside me, its doing it's damndest to explode from every cell in my body at once. I've tried a few times to mimic what he does and says in my day-to-day life, in the hope that some of his stillness would rub off on me. So far, no luck.

"Liz, I can hear you thinking from here."

I shivered at the sound of his voice. It's an automatic response after the two months we've been seeing each other. Master Gareth speaks, my pussy gets damp, and I have to fight the impulse to drop to my knees.

Oh yeah, I figured out the whole submissive thing. I think I'm pretty much a poster child.

The flogger makes a soft hiss as it cuts through the air before hitting my naked back. Shit, that didn't even hurt. Nothing more than a love tap to get my attention. Okay, okay, I really needed to focus.

I could turn my head and catch a peek of him, but that would be going against tonight's rules. I'm not supposed to look his way until I've earned the right. Mind you, he tends to change the rules on me about halfway through. He's such a tease.

It's one of the things that I've grown to love about him.

Not that I'd tell him that. Holy shit, no way. If I'd learned anything in the two months we'd been together, it was that declarations of love would freak him the hell out.

My lips have grown dry and I wanted nothing more than to wet them with my tongue. I won't, though. Not yet. Right now the only thing I need to worry about is concentrating on him.

"Sorry, Sir."

"What are you thinking about?"

Christ, of course we're going to have to play the honesty game tonight. "I was wondering how you can always be so still and quiet when I'm ready to run a marathon."

His chuckle does things to my body that shouldn't be possible without physical contact. I'm pretty certain I could come simply by listening to him speak. Maybe I could convince him to read one of those erotic books Connie has. Oh yeah, I would totally be able to sell tickets for that shit.

Actually no, no tickets. I've also come to the conclusion that I'm a wee bit jealous when it comes to Gareth. I was never good at sharing my toys. Right now, he's most definitely mine.

"Liz."

I squeezed my eyes shut and hoped I'd be able to resist the temptation to look. "I was also wondering if you'd read to me one night." No, sexy books wouldn't work. That would be crossing some weird sort of line he'd established for us. We do scenes, have coffee, and occasionally go to movies. But we're not *dating*. Not really. Is pre-dating a thing? If it is, then we totally had it nailed. "Maybe one of the novels you're teaching your class. I could read to you too. Maybe I could be your naughty student who didn't do her homework and needs to be punished."

The light scratch of his nails down my back dragged a surprised gasp from me. Normally I'm ticklish as hell, but when Master Gareth does that to me, laughing is the last thing I want to do.

What I really want is for him to fuck me.

Not that he's agreed to do that. Yet.

"I'm going to spank your ass now."

He knows that's my favorite thing for him to do. I've learned that I'm not quite a pain slut, but I do enjoy the burn that comes with a solid slap to the butt. A nice leather belt gets me fired up to the point where I could come with the slightest of touches to my clit, though I prefer his hand over anything else. There's nothing better than knowing the sharp bite of pain also made his hand sting from the contact. That it heats his skin as much as it does mine.

That maybe, just maybe someday it will drive him mad enough to want to fuck me.

Spend the night with me.

Be with *me.*

Master Gareth pulled my ass cheeks apart, kneading the flesh as he exposed my hole. His hot breath cooled the sweat that had collected on my back from the flogging. He'd gone easy on me tonight, even though we'd done over a dozen scenes together and I'm not so new to this any longer. I could always tell that he wanted more, wanted to take, and for some reason held back. Fuck, I think I've been more than clear about my intentions.

I wanted to have sex with him.

His cock in my cunt. Hell, I was at the point where I wanted to get a T-shirt made with that written on it.

Maybe it was worth one more chance.

I wiggled my ass and somehow managed to widen my knees without putting too much pressure on my clamped nipples.

"Please, Sir."

"Please what?"

"Please, will you fuck me?"

He stilled and his grip tightened on my ass. "Liz—"

"I'll do whatever you want. Be in any position. Please, Sir, I want you to take me. Fuck me. Push me into the mattress until I can barely breathe."

He leaned in and pressed his forehead to one of my ass cheeks. I hoped he'd say something, give me some kind of response so I could at the very least argue with him. But no, in typical Gareth fashion he said nothing.

Stubborn, insufferable—

The press of his tongue across my asshole had me moaning in a flash. I'd started getting Brazilians shortly after we'd begun playing and I realized how much he loved licking my pussy and rimming my ass. His tongue was wicked and Master Gareth was a man with few inhibitions. He would lick me anywhere he thought would get a reaction.

Yeah, it's really hard to stay mad at a man whose goal in life seems to be giving me the best orgasms I'd ever had.

He reached between my legs and dragged his fingers along the side of my clit, across the smooth skin of my pussy lips. Repeatedly, he stroked and probed without touching where I wanted him to. He loved depriving me of my pleasure as long as he could. The longer he kept me on edge, the better the release was in the end.

"What do you think about getting your hood pierced?"

Oh. Fuck. I'm fairly certain my cunt just gushed at the thought. "Yes, Sir."

"Yeah, I knew you'd enjoy that idea. It would hurt for a few weeks, but the things I could do to you afterward." He dove back in and licked my ass.

He shifted from rubbing around my clit to pinching it as he slipped his thumb into my cunt. It had taken me awhile to get used to being licked this way, exposed and helpless. With my hands tied I couldn't do much to either help him or, God forbid, try to stop him. I was completely at his mercy.

Exactly the way I wanted it.

With each swipe of his tongue, I inched closer to my orgasm. My thighs ached from the angle, my nipples throbbed from the clamps, my ass still burned from the strap and I loved it all. I wanted more.

"Gareth. Please."

He bit down on my ass cheek, slapping the other side three times hard. "Get up."

Shit, I broke rule one.

Again.

I'm such an idiot.

"Sorry, Sir."

Now, I don't care how easy they make it look in porn movies, getting up with your hands cuffed behind your back when you're half splayed out on the floor is *not* an easy thing to do. Add in the nipple clamps and you have to be damn careful not to roll the wrong way and tug something that shouldn't be tugged.

I wish I could say that I have it down to a science and that I'm graceful, but in reality I'm sure I'm giving a fairly accurate impression of a beached dolphin trying to squirm her way back into the water. I've learned enough to wiggle my knees closer together and use my chin as leverage. Sometimes I have the strength to simply pull my upper body up and end up on my knees. It depends on how long a session we've had.

I really needed to get enrolled into a yoga class so I could build up my core strength.

Tonight, I rolled onto my side, then my back before I was able to sit up. Kneeling from there is a bit easier and it gives me the advantage of being able to look at Master Gareth guilt free.

He'd sat down on a stool, his gaze locked on me as I scooted into the expected position. Gareth had come straight from the university to my place, so he hadn't taken the opportunity to change out of his black dress pants and his navy blue dress shirt. His brown hair was messy, which meant he'd been running his hands through it a dozen times. He only did that when he was stressed or worried about something, a tell of his that I'd picked up on quickly in our time together.

It was still weird seeing him dressed in anything other than leather when we are doing a scene. I'm sure no matter how many months passed, the memory of him coming up on the stage of the Tail Whip, offering himself up as part of a charity auction, will always be how I expect him to look.

The top three buttons of his shirt had been undone, revealing the dark chest hair I loved to touch and the strong column of his neck. He'd been sweating, too, from the exertion of the flogging and spanking, making his skin look richer in texture. His cock was hard and bulged out the front of his pants, a hidden delight.

It was the only reassurance I'd had that he really did want me.

Finally, when I got into the position I knew he wanted, I lowered my chin to my chest and waited. We'd been working on my training, even if he refused to call it that, and I knew what he expected. Strangely, that knowledge helped quiet my mind. All I needed to do was kneel and wait. He'd tell me what he wanted, or he'd take what he needed. My only task was to listen, react, let him take control and call the shots.

"I can't do what you want, Liz. Not yet."

There was something in his voice that drew my attention. He wasn't looking at me, his gaze locked on the floor. It was the hardest thing in the whole damn world not to say my safeword so he'd be forced to let me go. I wanted nothing more than to pull him into a hug to try to make things better.

Shit, I wasn't completely certain what was wrong, but I couldn't stand to see him this way. He was a good man and he deserved to be happy.

I wish he'd let himself be happy. . . .

"That's okay." I was surprised how shaky my voice sounded. "I didn't mean to push you, Sir."

"It's just—fuck it." Master Gareth growled. "You've been a good girl tonight. What do you want? Tell me one thing."

This wasn't the time to have a heart-to-heart—neither one of us was up for it. Which left me with only one answer.

"I want to suck your cock until you come."

Okay, so I'd learned not to beat around the bush with him. You can't blame a girl for being direct.

Master Gareth nodded and stood. Words can't describe how happy I was to see that his cock hadn't softened. He was still turned on and it was my job to make sure he got every bit of pleasure his body could handle.

I opened my mouth before he had taken himself out, which pulled a smile from him. "Greedy."

I hoped he could tell I was smiling inside my head.

The skin of his crown was soft as he dragged his cock along my bottom lip. "You've such a beautiful mouth."

I let my tongue slip out so I could taste him. The tip was already covered in precome, bitter and wonderful against my taste buds. It was hard not to lean in and suck him, but I didn't want to ruin things for either of us. Master Gareth had taught me that sex is the same as good food or wine—something to be savored, never rushed. Every moment spent with a lover is precious and shouldn't be squandered because you never know when you'll have another chance to be with them.

They could be taken from you in the blink of an eye.

I kept my gaze focused on his face and not on the treat before me. His brown eyes sparkled and his lips had turned up in a soft smile.

"Good girl. You're waiting and being patient. You should definitely get your treat."

He began to stroke his shaft, his hand going to the base of his fly, pushing the blood to the tip of his cock. His pants were still mostly in place and I couldn't see his balls or most of his pubic hair. Having sex with our clothes mostly on was a kink I never knew I'd had before I'd met him. Master Gareth exploited it now that he knew.

I stuck my tongue out and tried to beckon him closer. This time my silent begging worked. He shuffled closer and positioned his shaft in front of my waiting lips.

"Suck me."

Hell yes!

I closed my eyes, leaned in, and swirled my tongue around his head. There was another burst of precome, my warning that he was as turned on tonight as I was. This was one blow job that would be short in duration. Not that I knew *all* of his tells, hell, we haven't done this that much, but I've learned to pick up on the warning signs for when a man is about to fill my mouth.

Especially him.

One thing I knew he enjoyed was when I ran my tongue along the underpart of his head. That little bundle of nerves was a wonderful target to tease. If I moved my tongue just so . . . oh yeah. Fuck, I loved it when he moaned deep and low like that.

I didn't want him to come too quickly, so I slowed my pace. I'm not sure when extending his pleasure became so important to me, but it was. I think the more I learned about him, about the type of man Gareth was when he wasn't busy being a Dom, the more I realized he deserved every bit of happiness he could get.

Okay, so I took on more than I thought when I'd first invited him to coffee. I've never been one to back away from a challenge and I wasn't about to start now.

Plus, you know, that whole *I think I might love him* thing. I glanced up and for once I hoped he could see the depth of my feelings in my expression.

I know how I look while I'm sucking his cock, he made me look in a mirror once when I did it. I know what it does to him when he realizes I have my entire undivided attention focused on him. Shit, I wish my hands were free so I could grab him by the hips, pull him down my throat, and hold him there.

Never mind, I did the next best thing.

Humming Coldplay while giving head might not be considered a big turn-on by some, but it worked for me. And him. Master Gareth bucked his hips forward when I hit the high notes. I knew I had him the moment he grabbed me by the head and held me still. It took me a few times to get used to him doing this, expecting me to be perfectly still while he fucked my face. Not once have I ever felt used by him, less than the woman I am. If anything it gave me a sense of power. I reduced him to this—me, simple little Liz. I was a goddess on my knees.

"Fuck." His fingers dug into my head a moment before his come filled my mouth.

I tried my best to swallow down every drop, but let's be honest, that only happens in porn movies. A long string of cum slipped from my mouth to roll down my chin. It was messy and sticky and fuck, if it wasn't the best thing ever. I loved it. Loved him.

Best not to dwell on those feelings.

Master Gareth pulled out and yanked me to my feet. It took him a second to free my hands and rub some life back into them. The pins and needles sensation was one I'd always enjoyed. Now having someone not only willing to inflict the feeling on me in the best way possible, but also able to help chase it away afterward, made me one happy woman.

His tug on the chain currently linking the nipple clamps together brought me back to the moment. I looked up into his eyes and my mind simply stopped. The chaos that normally swirls around stilled as my heart rate doubled.

"You're such a good girl, Liz." He cupped my cheek and ran his thumb along the side of my nose. "I can't imagine—"

God, I hated when he did that. Yes, we had all these rules in place to make sure we're both protected, but I was tired of playing it safe. I wanted him to want me. I wanted him to need me.

I wanted him to finish those goddamned sentences.

Before I had a chance to complain, Master Gareth scooped me up and carried me over to the couch. My legs were pushed back and his head was between my legs before my brain had time to register it. A hand was wrapped around the chain between my breasts and he tugged as he licked me. He never gave me time to mentally catch up to what he did to my body.

It was fucking great.

My pussy was soaked from a combination of his saliva and my juices as he sucked my clit. I had no choice but to come. The throbbing pain from my nipples only served to add to the sensation, the overwhelming rush that exploded from me, obliterating everything that lay in its path.

For a few blessed moments, I wasn't Liz. There was nothing but the sensation or heat, pleasure and pain reducing me to my base elements.

It always took me awhile to mentally reassemble myself after Master Gareth took me apart. He never once rushed me, knowing that coming down in my own way had become a part of my process, moving from my sub headspace to my Liz headspace.

I didn't move when I felt him get up from the couch. Couldn't bother to open my eyes when I heard him zip up his pants and gather the blanket from the floor. The soft warmth was a welcome feeling after our session, and I had to fight the urge to burrow into it and drift off to sleep.

"Let me get those clamps off you."

Yeah, I whimpered. No matter how many times he used those damn things on me, getting them off sucked. Maybe I'm more sensitive there than some subs. I'm not sure. I just hope I'll get used to the sensation soon.

Oh, but he did use his mouth to soothe me when he took off the first one, then the other. There were perks to the pain. The aftercare was wonderful.

"Are you warm enough?" He pushed my hair from my face. I really should open my eyes, but I have something I wanted to ask him and I knew I wouldn't be able to if I had to look him in the eye.

"I'm good."

"Liz?"

"Don't you want to have sex with me?"

Somehow asking that simple question hurt more than the flogging. I really didn't want to consider why.

"I believe we both had orgasms."

I did open my eyes at that. Was he purposely being obtuse, or just trying to get me going? "That's not sex. Not the kind I'm talking about."

Gareth sighed and pinched the bridge of his nose. It was a sexy nose. I wished I had the energy to kiss it. "Liz, we've talked about this. I'm not ready for a relationship. Not yet."

"I understand that. And it's just sex."

He looked at me for several long moments. "It's not, though. I think you know that too."

Now, I knew that I was still new to the whole Dom and sub thing. I knew that doing a scene wasn't the same as having a romantic relationship. Connie and Stephen knew lots of people who were professional Doms who never once slept with their subs. But what we shared wasn't that.

We'd done coffee. Gone to movies. Hell, I'd been known to chat with him on the phone just to shoot the shit or bitch about how one of my coworkers is an idiot. That was a bit more than a professional relationship. Wasn't it?

I really wanted him to fuck me.

I wanted him to find the courage to take the next step with me.

I really didn't want to be alone anymore.

I cleared my throat and tried to smile. "It could be, though. Sex. We don't need to take things any further than that. It's just..." Somehow I managed to stop myself. "It's fine. I'm just sex addled."

"Liz—"

"Seriously. I'm happy." I just wish I could say the same about him. Gareth did so much for other people, but his own peace of mind seemed to elude him. I wanted to give back to him some of the joy he'd given to me.

I just didn't have a clue how to do that.

So, I nodded and did my best to keep my disappointment off my face. "Are you still marking exams?"

For a man who prided himself on his control, his face was an open book when he wasn't in Dom mode. His relief was apparent. "Only a few more essays to go, then I get to relax for a bit."

"Maybe we can do a movie then. There are actually a few good ones I've been itching to see."

He smiled at me then and I'm pretty damn certain if I'd been able to have a second orgasm I would have. "One of your action movies?"

"Of course!" I pulled the blanket up to my chin. "*Kaboom!*"

"Get some rest, crazy-head. I'll talk to you in a few days."

He kissed my forehead and moved to get his things. I would normally have gotten up and followed him around until he left, but I wasn't able to move. My busy brain had kicked back in and I'd begun pondering. I neatly labeled the issue *Gareth,* opened a mental file, and began to compile a list of my concerns.

I didn't remember hearing him leave.

CHAPTER 7

"You know, I think I might need to break things off with Gareth."

The plate Connie had been drying dropped to the sink with a crash as she spun around to glare at me. "What the hell are you talking about? You can't break up with him. You're perfect for each other."

Now, I always told Connie everything, it had been our thing since we became best friends. She'd heard all my frustrations, my fears, hell she knew when my period was going to start before I did. But I'd been a tiny bit terrified to say anything to her about this because I knew this was the reaction I would get.

I'd chosen to face this particular conversation sitting down. My coffee mug was hot enough to burn my hands, but I held on tight. A little bit of pain was always helpful when I was trying to focus. Something else Gareth had taught me.

Gareth.

I'd barely slept the night before as I mentally battled with myself over this. I knew I'd somehow let things get too emotional on my end. And he'd been clear from the start—at this stage he wasn't ready to get into a relationship. He wasn't saying never, just not right now.

I wanted now.

Why the hell was I so impatient?

"The thing is, he doesn't seem to want to move beyond what we have going. I mean, I don't really blame him. I can't imaging losing a partner the way he did. And I'm not looking to take her place or any-thing. But . . . God." I wasn't sure if he'd ever be ready to move on. And while I wouldn't expect a person would ever *get over* something like that, I hoped that after four years he might be ready to let someone else in.

Perhaps me.

God, I was so confused.

Connie flipped the dish towel over her shoulder, leaned back against the counter, and crossed her arms. "Okay, back up. What's the problem right now between the two of you?"

Really, talking about my period was less embarrassing than try-ing to converse about this with her. It would also have been more straightforward. "He doesn't want to have sex with me."

"Umm, hello. I've been kicked out of the bloody condo on more than one occasion because the two of you have been doing the nasty."

If only. "Well, he's been doing *things* to me."

"You say it as if it's bad."

"It isn't." God, was I really complaining about the fact that I'd been getting awesome orgasms? *Apparently.* "He's been helping me explore my limits and learn what I enjoy with this stuff. And I love talking to him."

"Then why the hell are you thinking about breaking up with him? That doesn't make even a little bit of sense."

"Because he won't have sex with me. Actually take his wonder-fully hung cock and put it into my very willing vagina. He'll go with-out coming before he'd do that to me and I don't know why." Actually, that was a lie. I knew exactly why he wouldn't fuck me—his deceased wife.

I'd never considered myself to be a jealous woman before now, but I couldn't deny that I held a small measure of that emotion to-ward a woman who I'm sure was a wonderful lady. Gareth loved her, still did, and I was scared there wasn't going to be any room for me inside his heart.

"This isn't really about sex, is it?"

"No." I took another big sip of coffee. "No matter what I do or say, I can't seem to make him happy. Not really happy. I was hoping that if we made love that maybe I could show him how awesome I think he is. How much I care for him."

Connie came over and fell into the chair across from me. "Stephen asked me the other day how I thought the two of you were making out. He's been worried about Gareth for months."

It had taken awhile for me to learn about Stephen and Gareth. They'd been friends for years, playing rugby together and coming into the scene around the same time. Where Gareth was quiet and thoughtful, Stephen was more showy and vocal. Connie loved that Stephen would let his Dom tendencies slip into their outside lives. She'd told me once that when he got possessive of her in front of other people, it made her feel special in a way she couldn't describe. I got that now that I've been with Gareth for a while.

Connie reached out and patted my hand. "Liz?"

"He's never talked about her or openly compared me to her. It's not as if he's being an asshole or anything. But I get the feeling he won't fuck me because it would be too much like cheating on her."

"She's been dead for four years. He needs to move on at some point."

I couldn't lie—I honestly hadn't been that deeply in love with anyone. It's not as though I was shallow or incapable of it, but before Gareth there hadn't been that spark of light that I'd felt with any of my previous boyfriends. The knowledge that with a few well-timed breaths, the spark would begin to blaze. It was something I wanted to experience.

Preferably with him.

"Do you really want to break up with him?" Connie reached across and took my hand. "If you do, know you have my support. Stephen knows him well enough to get it and won't be pissed either. Hell, he'll probably bitch Gareth out for upsetting you."

"Thanks."

Did I really want to do that? Walk away without another glance? It was the easy way out, a path that I wouldn't normally take.

When I was alone at night I would still imagine seeing Gareth for the first time, not when he was under the spotlight onstage at the charity auction, but when he was peeking out from behind the curtain. I thought he was the most beautiful man I'd ever laid eyes on. Now that I'd gotten to know him a bit better, my opinion had only strengthened.

I loved it when he'd smile. Not the ones he put on for show. No, it was when something would catch him off guard and he'd let out a surprised chuckle. That smile would reach his eyes, making them sparkle. More and more I started to see him that way, and every time I fell in love with him a bit more.

Did I really want to walk away? Or did I want to take a chance and see if I could light that spark inside him?

Screw that.

"No, I don't want to break up with him. I just don't know how to make this work."

Connie nodded once, giving my hand a squeeze. "Remember me telling you about my dog Andy?"

"The Lab?"

"Yeah. He was a pain in the ass. I loved that stupid mutt despite all the shit he would get into. We got to a point, though, where my parents wanted me to give him up. I made them a deal. I'd take Andy to dog training and they had to give me the time to try to make things right. It took a while, but Andy and I figured things out."

"You want me to take a Dom to obedience classes?" Wouldn't that be one for the papers?

Connie chuckled. "Well, no. Though that would be kind of hot. But a good Dom needs to learn as much about himself as he does his sub. From what Stephen has told me, Gareth has changed a lot since Rachael died. Maybe he needs to relearn who he is as a man as well as a Dom? It's easy to ignore what's wrong with yourself when you're focused on someone else."

Shit, I hadn't even considered that. "So, he's been using me to forget?"

"He hasn't been with anyone in four years. And from what Stephen said, Rache was his first serious relationship." Connie shrugged. "What we need is a plan. A way to help him see that it's okay for him to move forward in his life."

A plan for training a Dom.

It was almost as absurd as her idea to buy a Dom for a night.

Of course, that had turned out fairly well. What was to say this wouldn't either? I could show Gareth how much he meant to me, maybe encourage him to take our relationship to the next level and in the end bring us closer together. I just had to have big enough proverbial balls to do it.

I took another deep drink of coffee and waited for the pain to dissipate before I spoke again. "So, what do you have in mind?"

I don't think I ever remember seeing Connie give me such a devilish grin before. I should have known enough to start worrying.

*   *   *

The phone had grown warm in my hands as I turned it over. I was supposed to have called Gareth twenty minutes earlier, but I still couldn't figure out the right words to say to him. Sure, Connie and I had practiced the whole damn speech. I'd even gone over it again with Stephen when he got home from work. But that was a completely different thing from actually calling up Gareth and letting the words come out of my mouth.

Basically, I was a big chicken shit.

I hated being a chicken shit.

Close your eyes and just do it.

Yes, I actually closed my eyes when I pressed the speed dial for him. It was lame, but at this point I was willing to do anything to get through the call. I kept them closed, too, as the ringtone sounded three times before he picked up.

"Hey." The sound of his deep voice always did strange things to my stomach. And my pussy. Not to mention the way my heartbeat doubled.

God, I had it bad.

"Hey." I really wanted to giggle. I did that when I got nervous, but I knew I couldn't. Not if I was going to make this believable. "So, I wanted to ask you something."

"You're late calling. Everything okay?"

Shit. "Yes and no."

"That doesn't sound good." I could hear him shifting around, papers being rearranged. He was probably still at work. "Did you want to meet for a coffee? Talk?"

"No!" Oh, nice overreaction there, Lizzy. "I mean, you sound busy."

"Just grading midterms. I can duck out for a while."

"No, this isn't a *duck out* conversation." I closed my eyes again, enjoying the sudden lack of sight. "I was wondering if you're free this weekend?"

He didn't respond right away, and for a moment I thought I might have lost the call. But then I picked up his breathing—shallow—the sound of him swallowing, and I knew he realized how serious this request was.

"All weekend?" He was trying to gauge my emotions. He'd slipped into that slightly detached tone of his he used when we are doing a scene. Right now, the last thing I wanted was for him to slip into his Dom-space. I needed to talk to *Gareth*.

I realized my speech wasn't going to work. If I didn't change tactics quickly, I'd lose him.

"You make it sound like that would be a horrible idea."

"Not at all—"

"Because really I just wanted to, you know, hang out. It's like we haven't had a chance to do that in a while."

"Liz—"

"Well, we don't have to if you're busy."

"*Liz.*"

"Yes?"

"I could use some time away from thinking about half-baked theories on *The Importance of Being Earnest*. Plus, I'm never too busy for you."

Oh. God, he could be so sweet. "I was thinking that maybe we could do something a bit different than coffee or . . . other stuff."

I smiled at the sound of his chuckle. "What do you have in mind?"

"IKEA." It was that or the hardware store, and I didn't want to give him any ideas for new *play* equipment.

"Is this about those bookshelves you mentioned?"

"Connie threatened to kick me out of the apartment if I didn't get my collection under control. She and Stephen are going to Collingwood this weekend, so I thought it would be a good excuse to tidy up."

"And you need help?" He knew I was deflecting, but thankfully he didn't call me on it.

"I was looking more for company and the chance to hang, but if the idea of coming to my rescue will get you to tag along, then yes. Please, please, please, I need your help."

"Cheeky."

"I try."

I don't know why I thought this was going to be hard. Despite my tendencies to freak out for no reason, this was *Gareth*. Dom or not, we did connect on a level that had nothing to do with my enjoyment of him tying me up. Our friendship had taken me a bit by surprise at first, but we really did have a lot in common. It was the perfect foundation for a kick-ass relationship.

I simply had to make him aware of it too.

"What time are you thinking?"

I jumped to my feet and might have done a Snoopy dance. "How about six-thirty on Friday?"

"I'll pick you up."

"Awesome. Thank you."

"You don't have to thank me. You know I have a soft spot for you."

We chatted a bit longer, but my mind was already on what I needed to do next. While I really did want to go to IKEA, I needed to make a few other purchases beforehand. I had every intention of making Friday night one he wouldn't forget for a long time.

And if luck was on my side, maybe we'd be taking the next step in our relationship.

Or we'd be breaking up.

Only time would tell.

CHAPTER 8

"I think we might have destroyed my car's shocks." Gareth dropped the third of the large IKEA boxes onto the living room floor. "Was there anything else?"

His five o'clock shadow had come in, and I'd spent the better part of two hours trying to not stare. I knew he hated the scruffy look, but I thought it made him look amazing.

"Nope, I grabbed everything else." I'd actually gone nuts with the shopping, not at all what I'd intended. But I wasn't about to pass up the opportunity either. I mean, come on . . . IKEA!

Gareth stood in the middle of the room, his hands on his hips, surveying the pile of boxes and scattering of bags. "I'm almost scared to ask if you want help with this."

"Oh, would you?" I totally knew he would. "It would go a lot faster with two people and then I could spend tomorrow getting the books up and organized and Connie won't hate me quite so much. I promise I won't make you work the whole weekend either. I bought beer and we can watch a movie on Netflix later if you want." Netflix? Well, it was as good a plan B as anything. Hopefully, there wouldn't be a need for movies. Though any excuse to watch *Secretary* was good with me.

Gareth rolled up his sleeves and tore open the boxes. He'd worn jeans and a button-down shirt, my favorite combination on him.

Damn, I had to leave if I was ever to get phase two of The Plan into action.

"I have to hit the bathroom." I started edging my way from him. "Need anything before I disappear?"

"No, I'm good. I'm surprised you haven't exploded yet." He smirked at me before returning his attention back to the box. "How many coffees did you have?"

"Only two." That he saw. "I'll be out in a minute."

I'd gotten everything I'd need ready before he'd picked me up. My bathroom had been converted from the place I primp and clean into a leather works. I'm not normally one for all the trimmings, but I had to admit it was a lot of fun shopping with Connie. The thigh-high leather boots were my favorite of the outfit. The way the leather clung to my skin as I laced them up damn near made me come. Yet another kink I'd have to explore.

The corset and skirt left nothing to the imagination. I had to practice putting everything on a few times to make sure I could do it quickly. Honestly, my first few attempts at dressing were funny as hell. At least now I knew how to do it without ending up in knots.

With the strings tightened, boots on and panties off, I quickly put on the cherry red lipstick and darkened my eye shadow. I really didn't look myself, but that was the whole point. Pulling my hair into a tight bun changed the way my face looked. I was no longer sweet, funny, and slightly odd Liz. I'd morphed into Domme, Mistress Elizabeth.

So. Frigging. Weird.

And a little bit hot.

But this was the plan to help Gareth get past whatever this block was in his head. His wife wouldn't have wanted him to be alone. At least, I would hope not.

"Liz, do you have a hammer?"

"In the kitchen pantry. Third shelf."

I somehow managed to keep myself calm enough, listening at the door for him to go into the kitchen. Not that I had my entrance planned precisely, but this was a bit better than the cheesy *hey sexy, wanna fuck* bit I had in mind.

Holding myself back until I knew he was rummaging in my pantry, I tiptoed my way into the living room, pushing open the door to my bedroom on the way. I had practiced my pose—Connie insisted—so I knew exactly the impression I was giving.

Imposing. Sexy.

As long as I didn't laugh.

Please God, don't let me laugh.

"I don't know how you and Connie can find anything in that mess. I'm surprised Stephen hasn't made you—" Gareth stopped dead in the doorway, his eyes wide. "Whoa."

"Are you criticizing my organizational skills?"

I would have loved to have cocked an eyebrow the way he does when he's annoyed with me, but I can't do it. Instead, I narrowed my gaze and lowered my chin. I knew I got the look right when he sucked in a sharp breath.

"Liz, what are you doing?"

"That's Mistress Elizabeth. I'm the one in charge here tonight." Okay, so I actually sounded pretty good there. Liz on steroids or something.

Gareth smiled and gave his head a small shake. "I'm not sure I want to play this game, Liz."

"Believe it or not, this isn't actually about you. Now come here."

Stephen had let me borrow his riding crop from his toy box. He said it would add to the whole air of control, plus it would give me something to do with my hands. The downside was how sweaty my palm was getting as I had to wait to see if Gareth would come this far, trust me enough to at least hear me out.

Gareth pushed his wire-framed glasses up his nose. He always wore his contacts when we were doing a scene, but I loved seeing him in his glasses. It was another subtle change that I hoped would help make things work tonight. I didn't move—a feat in itself—as I waited. He was always more patient than me, but I could see the cracks in his resolve tonight.

This was different. I'd not only caught him off guard, but I'd nudged him into unfamiliar territory. From what Stephen had told me that was something very few people had ever been able to do.

When he took that first step toward me, I wanted to jump and whoop. I bit the inside of my cheek and tightened my grip on the crop instead.

"Liz?"

I narrowed my gaze again.

"I mean, Mistress Elizabeth?"

"Not another word until you come here." Stephen's crash course on being dominant had been helpful, but most of what I needed to know I'd learned from Gareth himself. The way he handled me, how he kept himself composed, how still he could be. That was the type of Domme I wanted to be for him. I had a feeling he needed it more than most.

I could smell his cologne and the faint whiff of sweat from having moved the heavy boxes up from the car as he drew closer to me. Normally, I'd be the one begging to lick the side of his neck, needing to taste him. It was oddly arousing to be on the other side of this power exchange.

Tonight it was my job to look after Gareth, to make sure that he knew he was as safe with me as I was with him. To give back to him the gift he gave so freely to me.

Gareth still hesitated, but after a few more moments he sauntered over to me. I could tell by the way he moved he wasn't convinced that I was serious about this whole thing, but he was willing to play along for the time being. He stopped half a foot from me and grinned.

Wearing these boots, I was nearly as tall as him. I don't know if the added few inches gave me more confidence, or if I was actually starting to slip into the role. Instead of my normal lip-biting routine, I lifted my chin and evenly met his gaze.

"On your knees."

He did cock an eyebrow then—God, I wish I could do that—but didn't otherwise move. Now, Liz would have been tempted to throw a "Please, Sir" on the end of that command. But right now I was Mistress Elizabeth and I wasn't about to be begging for anything. Without looking away from him, I flicked the crop so I landed a smack to the outside of his thigh.

"Now."

It was weird. One moment we were standing there as equals. I had asked in the strangest way possible for him to trust me and go along with what I had planned. Though he didn't actually say the words, I knew he understood. I was then forced to stand by and watch him work his way through his decision. God, I could practically see his thought process running through his mind as he weighed the pros and cons, the benefits of going along for the ride.

I must look this way to him too. Even more so.

Connie always told me the power actually lies with the sub in these situations, but I never quite believed her. Not until this moment when I realized if he said no, or made any indication that he wasn't into what I was about to do, that I'd have to walk away. I might be the one with the crop, but that wasn't true power.

Shit, I hadn't considered that he might say no. This wasn't something we'd ever discussed before and despite Stephen's reassurances, I didn't know for certain if he'd be into this.

Plan C—we'd have to have a *conversation*. Not sure how that would go.

Gareth cocked his head to the side and let his gaze run down my body. I wanted to preen, but that, too, wouldn't have worked. Mistress Elizabeth wouldn't care what a sub thought of her appearance. She was a bastion of power and control. Queen of the bedroom.

I sighed and tried to look bored. He chuckled again. But after a few more seconds, he sank slowly to his knees.

Oh.

Oh yes, please.

I moved behind him, careful not to touch any part of his body, but needing to get out of his line of sight for a few moments. While I had no problem taking charge at the office when I needed to, this was different. I mean, Gareth had always projected that quiet core of steel, one that I didn't think could be dented, let alone broken.

Standing there, with him on his knees, I started to wonder exactly how wrong I was.

I let out a huff and did my best to push the distracting thoughts from my mind. I had only one thing to focus on right now and that was the man at my feet.

"You have been hiding yourself from me." I lightly tapped the back of his head with the crop. "I'm not sure if you thought I was dumb or if I wouldn't call you on it, but I've had enough."

"Liz, I—"

The fabric of his pants increased the sound of the crop landing against his ass, even though I knew it would dull the sensation. It didn't stop him from jumping or twisting around to look at me. I'd surprised him, and I could tell from his eyes that he hadn't been taking Mistress Elizabeth seriously.

Oh, dude, that was mistake number one.

"Take your shirt off."

It was funny how I found myself trying to emulate what Gareth did to me. Voice calm and steady, free from emotion. I kept out of his line of sight and touched him only when I wanted to get a reaction. I made him wait until the limits of his resolve were tested.

The bastard had more patience than me, but that didn't mean I couldn't do this.

I gave the top of his shoulder a tap with the crop, a bit harder than maybe I should have, when he didn't react. "I said, shirt off."

Gareth let out a shuddering breath. Slowly, he started undoing the buttons of his shirt. Inch by inch, his body was revealed to me. Firm skin and tight muscles as the fabric dropped down his arms and finally to the floor. I couldn't stop myself from running the leather tip of the crop along the back of his shoulders, down the curve of his spine to the top of his waistband.

"Very nice." I counted to five in my head, took a breath, and moved around him until I stood in front of him once more. "Excellent in fact."

"Thank you."

I lifted his chin with the crop and waited for him to correct his mistake.

"Thank you, Mistress."

Yeah, I could get used to this.

"I've noticed you're not very good at listening. I plan on teaching you how to be better at it. What do you have to say about that?"

Gareth didn't say anything. Okay, not exactly the response I wanted, but I couldn't let his stubborn streak get to me. "See, this is exactly what I'm talking about. Not listening. I asked you a question. I'm waiting for a response."

He kept his eyes up and locked onto mine. There wasn't the normal calm I was used to seeing in him. Holy shit, he actually looked a little freaked out. I knew I was supposed to stay in character, but I couldn't, not with him barely keeping it together. I reached down and cupped his face in my hands, letting the crop fall to the floor.

"We can stop this right now." I leaned in and kissed his forehead. Gareth sucked in a sharp breath, but he didn't otherwise move. "I . . . I probably got this all wrong. I got the impression you might enjoy having someone else in charge for once. Give you a bit of a break. And I wanted to show you that I could actually do this . . . and I wanted to just . . ."

I pulled back enough to watch him swallow. His eyes were filled with unshed tears and his hands were shaking as they hung limp by his side. Dammit, this wasn't right at all. I can't believe I'd screwed things up so badly this fast.

"Gareth, I'm sorry. I didn't mean to upset you. Let's just forget that I—"

"Thank you."

I was so surprised I'm sure I gave an excellent gaping-fish impression. "What?"

He reached up and placed his hand over mine. "I don't think I've ever had anyone do something so . . . generous for me before."

That's right, that's me. Good old generous Liz. "*What?*"

Gareth chuckled, but he made no move to run away screaming. Hell, he somehow went from looking panicked to relaxed in the space of a few heartbeats.

"Liz, you're not a Domme."

"Believe me, I know. But Stephen said you needed to have things shaken up a bit, and Connie wanted me to ask you to participate in an orgy, but I was pretty sure you wouldn't be into that. I thought this might be a better option. So I bought the outfit and borrowed the crop and I really wanted to give you a special night as a thank you for everything you've done for me. And maybe see if there was possibly a chance that we could take things a bit further."

Whoa, he didn't interrupt my tirade.

He wasn't saying anything, in fact.

"Gareth?"

"Yes, Mistress?"

Okay, so if I thought I was wet before, having this in-control, domineering man call me Mistress had me nearly coming on the spot.

"Do you want me to continue?" I gave his cheek a gentle squeeze. He was always doing that to me, touching and caressing. It settled me in a way I hadn't realized contact could. If luck was with me, it would do the same for him. "Because for a minute there it looked as if you were freaking out. I need you to say the words so I know I'm not forcing this on you."

Gareth didn't have the same tells that I did. He didn't lick his lips or bite his cheek when he got nervous. But surprisingly, he would drop his gaze. An odd thing given what he enjoyed doing in the bedroom. Though I've come to the realization that who we are when the door closes doesn't encapsulate everything about us as a person.

Currently, Gareth was staring at a spot on my chest—probably my cleavage. It was a really nice corset and did its job spectacularly.

"Yeah, I think I do."

There was that internal Snoopy dance going on again.

"What's your safeword?"

"Book."

"Book? Really? That's very . . . *book?*"

"Don't make fun of the safeword, Liz."

"Right. Sorry. Book, it is."

I had to step away then and give myself a minute to get back into character. I also knew that he'd need a few moments of quiet himself. It really is a different headspace when you're doing a scene, even if it's with someone you care about. Especially then. The last thing you wanted to do was fuck it up and hurt them.

As weird as this was, I wanted to show him that I could be the woman he could trust to take the next step with. The only way I could think to do that was to pretend to be something I wasn't, to give him something he needed.

I loved him enough to make the effort.

Starting up my saunter around him once more, I made sure to scoop up the riding crop from where it had fallen. The leather wrap around the handle had cooled down, but it wouldn't be long before we had it hot and sweaty once more.

It was time.

I had a Dom to train.

CHAPTER 9

The apartment was hot. I'd turned up the temperature when Gareth had been bringing the bookcases up from the car. The last thing I wanted was for him to be cold, but holy shit, I might have put it up a few degrees too high. A fine prickle of sweat lined his bare shoulders, making them glisten in the low light.

He'd been on his knees, waiting for me to finish my poking and prodding for the past fifteen minutes. If our positions were reversed, I'd have been totally freaking out in my head. It doesn't sound as if it's a long time, but when you have someone standing over you and you're completely at their mercy, oh yeah, it's a lifetime and then some.

Honestly, I had been biding my time as I mentally went over everything Stephen told me I should do. I wasn't experienced at using whips, paddles, and canes, and there was a real possibility that I could hurt him if I did something wrong. Gareth had been too good to me over the months for me to screw up and do him harm.

Slow and steady won the kinky race.

"Stand up and take your pants off." I hadn't realized how dry my mouth had gotten. I think this was probably the longest I'd gone not speaking in recent memory. I hate silence and can't resist the compulsion to fill it.

Gareth loved the calm. I had been fascinated to watch his muscles tense and relax as the minutes ticked on. He jumped at the sound of my words, but moved to comply.

"Make sure you fold everything and place it on the chair. I don't want your shit everywhere." God, that was bitchy. Go me!

"Yes, Mistress."

I growled as he walked away from me, his perfect, naked ass swaying as he went. *Am I this way? Vulnerable and sexy?* The urge to care for him warred with my need to spank his ass, turning it red.

Maybe I had a bit of Domme in me after all.

He placed his clothes on the chair and was about to turn around. "Stop!"

A ripple passed through him and his ass clenched.

As if he knew what was coming. Maybe he did.

"You have a very nice rear end. I want to see more of it." Amongst other things. "Bend over and put your hands on the arms of the chair. Stick that ass out for me to examine."

He'd put me in a similar position once. It was during our second scene, the first one out of the club. We'd gone back to his place where he'd gotten things ready ahead of time. The only thing in his living room was a sturdy wooden chair and a paddle. That had been a great night.

Walking up behind him now reminded me of how turned on he'd been then. I'd thought he was going to fuck me so hard I'd feel it for days. Instead, he'd fucked my mouth, making me swallow his come. That wasn't how I'd wanted that particular evening to end.

Tonight, I would change the outcome to something more suitable.

I ran my hand down his side to the small of his back, before cupping his ass cheek. I gave it a squeeze, letting my nails dig into the flesh and leaving marks behind. Gareth sucked in a quick breath, but he held still.

"Do you enjoy that?" I squeezed the other cheek and then raked my nails down the flesh. "I now understand the appeal of being able to mark you. I'm leaving such pretty pictures in your skin. I could scratch my name there and watch it soak back in. My mark, my claim on you."

Fascinated with the red lines, I continued to make lines across the expanse of his back, his ass, the back of his thighs. The hair on his legs caught on my nails, tickling the sensitive skin beneath. The longer I continued, the more his body began to shake. Typical Gareth, he took everything with his normal quiet demeanor.

I needed to shake things up.

"You're being such a good boy. But I don't think you're appreciating what I'm doing for you."

He turned his head and peered at me over his shoulder. "What?"

I gave his ass a slap so hard my hand stung. "Pardon?"

He gasped, but his gaze didn't leave mine. "I'm sorry, Mistress."

"That's better." I went back to scratching his skin. "Now, what I was saying was you aren't showing your appreciation for what I'm doing. I want you to *talk*. Tell me what you're feeling as I do things to you."

Ah, there it was, a little flash of panic. Stephen said Gareth had held things too tightly for years. He needed a push to get him out of that dark shell and back into the light of day.

"If you can't do that, then this can stop right now. Go ahead and use your safeword. I don't mind." I pulled back at the same time he grabbed for my hand.

"Please, stay. I'll try, Mistress."

Without waiting for my response, Gareth resumed his position, even widening his stance. My heart pounded as my brain finally caught up to everything we'd been doing. Yeah, I know I'd planned this, but planning and doing are two very different things.

A deep breath. Start with the basics, with what you know and everything will come up aces.

I moved so I stood behind him, but slightly to the side. "Start talking." I punctuated my words with a slap to his left cheek.

Gareth groaned. "It stings, but you didn't hit me too hard. You aimed a bit too low for it to really make an imp—"

I spanked him three times as hard as I could manage. He cried out as he squeezed the arms of the chair. "It wasn't an invitation to critique my technique. Tell me what you're thinking. Feeling."

"It hurts. I'm not used to feeling pain this way. I haven't been on this side of things before."

There we go.

I moved to his other side, knowing how things could change from a good pain to a bad pain if the blows weren't spread out a bit. Another three slaps and his skin started to take on a light red color.

"I didn't think I'd enjoy being spanked. I'm still not sure if it's my thing. But I love your hands on me."

I could tell he was starting to sink down into his head a bit. That first time between us at the charity auction had been my first experience with what Connie called sub-space. It was weird and freeing, a type of mental numbness that allowed you to turn your brain off and simply exist for a while. As much as he teased me about not having a switch in my head, I did. It seemed he did too.

Another thing we had in common. Another connection.

Instead of continuing the spanking, I dropped to my knees behind him and bit his ass. Now, when I did something similar as a sub, Gareth enjoyed directing me. He never let me play where I wanted, do to him what I really wanted to do.

His body was clean, but the scent of recent sweat clung to him. I licked across the cheek, enjoying the feeling of his fine hairs against my tongue. Fuck, he'd stopped talking again. I bit down hard enough to pull a yelp from him.

"Christ, that hurt."

"Tell me."

The growl that came from him was clearly his Dom self wanting to come out to play. I gave him a little slap to remind him that Mistress Elizabeth was here instead.

"Tell me."

"I wish I could see what you're doing. I want to see the expression on your face as you're on your knees. I love seeing you on your knees."

Oh.

I squeezed his cheeks hard with my hands, taking a moment to fight off the unexpected rush of emotions. *Don't lose it now, Liz. Work to do.*

Now, I hadn't done a lot of extreme things with Gareth in our time together. Nothing that people who are more experienced in the lifestyle than I am would consider *out there*. But there are lines Gareth has pushed me past that I'd never considered going across before.

It was about time I did some pushing of my own.

Spreading his ass cheeks, I leaned in and nipped along the inside ridge of his ass. The muscle tensed hard beneath my teeth and he tried to stand up.

"Don't you dare!" My words were hot against him, bouncing back to echo in my ears. "I didn't say you could move."

"Liz, I—"

"Are you safewording on me? Over a little rim job?" I could tell that caught him off guard. "Get your hands back on those arms and don't move."

Apparently, Mistress Elizabeth *really* wanted to do this.

Who knew?

With my hand on the small of his back, I pushed him down and encouraged his legs wider. His cock, which was hard, hung heavy between them. Leaning in, I ignored the voice in my head that was freaking out about the fact that this couldn't be sanitary and licked a swipe along the back of his balls and along his perineum.

The skin and the smell weren't what I was expecting. The overwhelming scent of Gareth washed over me, the same bitter saltiness coated my tongue that did when I sucked his cock.

"God, that feels so good."

The problem with being a sub pretending to be a Domme is that it's really easy to lose yourself and forget your role. I mean, I'm not ashamed to admit I get off on getting *him* off. I love when I can cause those little slips in his control by doing exactly what he wants. So having him slip and become a moaning mess as I lick and nip my way along his balls and ass was heady shit.

"Touch my cock, Liz."

And then everything snapped back.

I pushed him forward, more in an attempt to get separation than to punish him. I was surprised to find that I shook nearly as much as he did. We'd both let our control slip and had briefly forgotten our new roles.

"I think you've forgotten who's in charge here tonight." I licked my lips, the taste of him still lingering. "You don't have permission to tell me what to do."

Gareth squeezed his eyes shut and chuckled. "Yes, Mistress."

"You forgot."

"Yes, Mistress. I did."

"If you're not going to follow the rules when I try to do something nice for you, then you're not going to have the treat."

Wisely, Gareth didn't respond.

"I think it's time we changed things."

Gareth cocked an eyebrow.

The poor man. He didn't have a clue what was in store for him. "I think it's time we took things to the bedroom."

*   *   *

Connie really was the best friend a girl could have. When we came up with this idea, she immediately went off on a rant of, *here's exactly what I would do to Stephen if I had a chance.* I hope it never comes to that between them, because I'm not sure Stephen would survive. Once she got past her own fantasies, she helped me plan out what I was going to do for Gareth.

More importantly, she helped me set everything up.

The man in question was currently trailing behind me, buck naked. He'd been surprisingly quiet since I'd suggested the bedroom. Maybe this was where he was having his own mental freak-out, knowing that I wanted to have sex with him. But proving once again that he was a stronger person than me, he didn't say anything about it.

"I want you on your knees at the foot of the bed, hands behind your head and eyes down." Gareth nodded, but that wasn't what I wanted. I managed to land a smack on his ass as he moved past me. "What was that? I didn't hear you."

"Yes, Mistress."

I think I might have preened a bit.

"You have been a bad boy. Not listening to my commands. Questioning my authority. Trying to take over. I don't know what your other Dommes have tolerated, but I won't put up with a toppy sub."

I was impressed he managed not to laugh.

"It occurs to me that even though you're a Dom, you haven't had the proper training. You've learned everything ad hoc. I intend to show you exactly what it means to be a sub so you will understand."

He looked up at that, a frown pinching his face. "I understand, Liz."

Okay, time to drop the mask for a second. "No, I don't think you do. You try to. You are generous and kind and have somehow managed to worm your way into my head faster than anyone else I've ever known. But you don't *understand.* You will, though."

I had to look away from him as another rush of emotion rolled through me. Dammit, why couldn't I do this for him without turning into some sort of basket case? God, I would be a mess if it turned out his feelings for me weren't the same as mine toward him.

Connie had put everything we'd discussed on my dresser and had covered it with a tea towel. The blue-and-white-checkered pattern hid the tools I was going to do my best to use. Flicking the towel away with a single swipe, I tossed it over my shoulder and stared down.

"What to choose, what to choose?"

It was all an act. I knew exactly what I wanted to use on him first, the order of the other items would follow in due course. There really was an advantage to having experienced the sensations from all of those things before.

First things first. Restraints.

"Stand up and walk over to the closet. Open the door." I actually had to stop myself from throwing a "please" on the end. It really didn't feel right bossing him around. *It's only one night, Liz, suck it up.*

I kept my back to him, remembering all the times when he did that to me. The feeling of wanting his attention but knowing I'd never get it if I didn't do exactly what he said. It was weird how important one person's opinion could become when everything else had been stripped away.

The squeak of the closet door being pulled open, followed by a soft snort had me smiling. I was still holding the riding crop and had to rearrange a few things to make room for it.

"Before you ask, it's Stephen's personal St. Andrew's Cross." Did I mention I love Stephen as much as Connie? "I think you know how that thing works. Get yourself set up on it as best you can. I'll do the rest."

I forced myself to count to thirty in my head after he finally stopped moving. God, this was almost as good as opening a Christmas present! I couldn't wait to turn around and see the look on his face, the flush on his skin. I grabbed the first thing I planned to use on him and stuffed it into my cleavage.

Making sure my eyes were actually open, I smiled as I turned to saunter toward him. "See, you're getting better at following directions already."

There was that glorious ass again. Gareth had stretched out along the cross, his hands coming up high enough he could cup the top of the wood. The restraints were simple Velcro cuffs attached to ropes. When Stephen first brought the homemade cross home, I couldn't get my head wrapped around what they would use it for. Yeah, accidently walking in on your friends while they are playing will really enlighten you.

"I'm going to tighten you up." I touched his shoulder before I made a grab for the cuff. Gareth would do that with me—touching to make sure I knew what was going to happen. Well, he did in the beginning until he broke me in. "I know we haven't talked about limits yet. Is there anything I should know? Anything to stay away from?"

"Liz, I don't think there is anything you could do to me that would push my boundaries."

"Still, I need to know. You have to say the words." Okay, so I knew he was right, but this was as much about reassuring him as it was setting limits. I needed him to know that I cared about him and what happened. Otherwise, this whole evening would lose its significance and meaning.

"No scat, golden showers, or blood. I don't mind bruises, but not to my face. Everything else will be fine."

"And what's your safeword again?"

"Book."

God, he was such a nerd.

I managed to get him secured without coming across as the amateur I was. The boots gave me the added height I needed to lean in without touching him. When everything was done, I walked around the cross so he could see my face. I must have had an odd expression on my face, because he was frowning again.

"Wondering what I'm going to do to you?" I didn't bother to wait for him to answer, and reached between my breasts and pulled out the nipple clamps I'd shoved there.

"Shit," he muttered, and closed his eyes.

"There's an expression. Something about turnabout and fair play? Ever heard of it? No?"

He thumped his head on the side of the cross. "Yes, Mistress."

"Now, if I remember correctly, I need to get you ready before I just clamp them on. How do I do this again? Right." Leaning in, I sucked on the closest nipple, ignoring the way he tried to jerk away from me.

The nub grew hard beneath my tongue as I teased it with my tip. Even when I closed my eyes I could feel his muscles straining as he fought against my moist attack, wanting to pull away, but unable to. Only when I thought he wouldn't be able to take another swipe did I pull back to admire my handiwork.

"That looks beautiful."

The nipple clamps Connie had let me use were different from the normal ones Gareth used. I took a deep breath, wiped off the saliva that still lingered on his skin, and slipped the clamp in place. I didn't have a lot of skin to work with, and honestly, I was a little freaked out that I'd do this wrong and hurt him in the not good way. But the BDSM gods must have been smiling down on me because I was able to slip the first one in place.

"How does that feel?"

"It fucking hurts. *Mistress.*"

I stood up straight and couldn't stop the grin from coming. "Excellent. Time for number two."

He groaned but couldn't do anything to stop me from tormenting him again. The second clamp went on with no difficulty, partly due to my newfound confidence and partly because Gareth was smart enough to stop moving.

Payback. Thank you, universe.

"Ouch." Gareth's growl was almost cute.

Time for phase two.

"That first night we met, I was pretty naïve about a lot of things. I'd heard about nipple clamps, but I hadn't used any. Hell, I'd barely dipped my toe into the kinky pool and you had me trussed up and clamped tight before I could say *whoa, Nelly.*"

I tried not to run back to my dresser to get the next item on my Gareth torture list, though I might have possibly skipped a bit. The paddle I'd picked out myself. It was one of my personal favorites that left a sting that melted into my muscles whenever he worked me over.

"I was so curious and more than a little nervous that it didn't occur to me to be scared. You were a complete stranger and for all I knew you would tie me up and do things to me that I wouldn't enjoy. I'd even paid for the pleasure."

Once more behind him, I ran my hand down along the swell of his ass. The pink from earlier had gone, leaving the skin pale and unblemished. I was going to have to do something about that.

Gareth was breathing heavily and his chin had dropped to his chest. I knew he was fighting through the pain, trying to control the surge of sensations flooding him. It wasn't going to work. Control wasn't what he needed tonight. He had to relax into it, accept the pain for what it was and let it flow through him.

"You showed me things that I didn't even know would turn me on. You taught my body that it was capable of more things, surviving more, enjoying sensations that I wouldn't have thought pleasurable."

I made sure I was standing in the right spot and that I was holding the paddle the way Stephen had showed me. It was heavier than I remembered it being, and my muscles in my biceps and shoulder pulled as I lined it up with his ass.

"You also helped me turn my brain off. I'm always thinking things ten steps ahead, worrying and wondering. I can't do that when you have me bound and clamped. I don't know, it's as if when you've got me pinned down, my brain has permission to switch off for a bit. I want to give that to you, give you that gift so you can understand, too."

I wasn't really prepared for the vibrations up my arm when the paddle connected with his ass. The sound was impressive to say the least. I was so used to being the one to feel the effects that went along with that noise, my pussy had dampened. Pavlov was a jerk and really frigging smart.

Gareth groaned. Yeah, I recognized that noise, too. It's the one I made when he'd pushed a bit too hard, too fast and I needed a few minutes to adjust. He never gave it to me.

I made sure the second slap landed in the same spot.

"Tell me what you're feeling." Oops, there was that Dom growl again from him. I made sure to land two smacks to his other ass cheek. "I don't hear you talking."

"It fucking hurts."

"More." Another smack.

"It burns. Really burns. I didn't think it was that intense." *Smack.* "Fuck! My dick and balls are tingling." *Smack.* "Dammit, Liz."

"Not Liz. Not tonight."

I landed three more spanks with the paddle before tossing it aside so I could admire the result. Not too bad for an amateur—self high five. His skin was nice and red, without a trace of white to be found. Gareth was panting, leaning heavily on the cross. I could tell he was in that stunned awareness phase, where your brain is trying to catch up to all the sensations your body threw at you.

Embracing my newfound inner bitch, I raked my nails down his ass. "I think I understand why you enjoy spanking me so much."

My hands shook, which threw me. Sure I was turned on seeing him in this position, but I didn't think I would react so strongly. And shaking hands right now was bad because I wanted to try the flogger. The last thing I wanted was to miss my mark.

Ah, fuck it. I'd make it work.

The flogger I'd picked out wasn't one that would cause a great deal of harm if I was careful. Honestly, it was one of my favorites for Gareth to use on me. It was only fair that I show him firsthand what the appeal of it was.

I walked around the front of the cross, needing to make sure he was still okay. A peek down to his nice hard cock told me everything I needed to know. Hands still warm? Yup. Gareth slowly becoming a drooling mess? Oh yeah.

All going according to The Plan.

I held up the flogger and tapped the end of his nose with it. "Exactly how horny are you right now?"

He looked up and I don't think I could ever remember his eyes being that dark before. "I could fuck you through the floor." He licked his lips. "Twice."

"Excellent." Hell yes, I was grinning. "No coming until I say you can. I'm going to flog you now."

"You're not being Mistress Elizabeth anymore. This is Liz I'm seeing."

Of course he would pick up on that. "I believe Mistress Elizabeth can act however the hell she wants. If that means I get to be excited about being able to flog my man, then I'll be excited."

Gareth had the nerve to roll his eyes. "Yes, Mistress."

I gave the chain linking his nipple clamps a solid tug before moving around behind him. "Don't be a jerk or I'll get out the butt plug."

"You know, there will eventually be payback for this."

"God, I hope so."

I widened my stance and gave the flogger a few tentative swings to get the feel for it. I'd briefly practiced last night on a pillow, which was weird. Yes, I kept calling it a bad pillow as I beat it. Sue me.

With my first swing I connected the leather tendrils against his right shoulder blade. Barely a love tap, but enough to get both our heads into the game. Making a figure eight with my hand, I landed a second strike to his other shoulder blade, a little firmer than the first.

"You know how much I enjoy our times together, right? I mean, I have earth-shattering orgasms and my throat is sore from the screaming afterward, so I'd assumed you knew." The next few swings were harder still, as I aimed for his ass. Gareth flinched, bucking his hips forward.

"Liz—"

"You've shown me so much in a short time. I don't think you realize how awesome I feel after we've been together. I float for days and people actually comment on my mood. Nothing at work can bother me. I get myself off at the thought of you standing over me, flogger in hand, and that look in your eye."

Gareth groaned and I could see light pink marks rising up along his back. Fuck, if I didn't get off soon, I was going to explode right here.

No. The one thing I'd learned from Gareth early on was the need for patience. He never did anything to me solely for his own pleasure. He always gauged my needs, desires, calculating what he wanted to give to me, when. He made sure that we both walked away satisfied.

Except for the no fucking part.

The only way I would get off tonight was with his cock buried deep inside me. And the only way *that* would happen was if he finally gave in and told me it was what he wanted.

"Liz . . . God."

Shit, this was too good. I dropped the flogger, moved around to the front of him, and dropped to my knees. His cock was hard and I could smell his arousal. At least tonight he couldn't deny me this pleasure.

Leaning in, I placed a kiss to the head, licking the precome from the tip. That familiar taste sent warmth racing through my body to all the right spots. I opened my mouth wide and with no preamble sucked as much of his cock as I could.

Gareth groaned and his body vibrated. Once more he fought against the restraints, but I knew it wasn't to get away from what I was doing to him. He wanted to grab my hair, fuck my face, and claim me for his. Yeah, this would be awesome.

I tightened my lips over my teeth as I drug myself back up his shaft. With his legs spread out, I had good access to his balls and ass again.

Now that I knew how much he enjoyed that, there was no sense in holding back. I shifted my face so I could run my tongue over his perineum.

"Liz, I can't take much more of this."

Neither could I.

"Liz, please. Let me come."

"No." I nipped at his inner thigh.

"*Please.*"

I let myself fall to the floor so I could look up into his face. It was the weirdest thing, seeing that look of unrepressed desperate lust on his face. Gareth who was always so tight with his emotions. Gareth, the man who even when he laughed it was little more than a chuckle.

This man bound to the cross who was flushed, bright eyed, and panting barely resembled the Dom I knew. Sweat rolled down his face and his hair was plastered to his scalp. The thick cock I loved so much bobbed with the rhythm of his heartbeat, showing how fast his blood rushed through him.

"You want to come?" I ran my finger down the side of my neck to my cleavage.

"Yes." The single word was little more than a whisper.

"What will you do if I let you down off that cross?"

"Anything."

I grinned. "Perfect."

CHAPTER 10

I got up and released his handcuffs, doing my best to keep steady on my feet. Between my shaking hands and his balled fists, the Velcro was initially uncooperative and I had to try several times to get it to cooperate even a little.

"I'll do the other. Get on your bed." His voice had gotten low, domineering. Not the pliant and submissive man I wanted him to be.

"No." I stepped away, leaving him still fastened tight. "I'm in control tonight. You'll do what I want or you'll damn well stay secured to this cross."

"What the hell, Liz?" Gareth tried to yank his hands out of the cuffs, but the Velcro held fast. "Let me go."

"Not until you promise me that you're going to keep playing by my rules. You gave me control tonight. Me. I'm the one looking after you making sure everything is fine. I thought you trusted me to do that?"

I would never have admitted it to him, but if Gareth said he didn't trust me the way I trusted him, I would let him off the cross and ask him to leave. Then I'd lose his phone number in my Deleted Items folder. Great sex is awesome, but I wanted a relationship, and I wouldn't settle for anything less than a mutually satisfying one.

Deep down, I knew he wouldn't let that happen. The sex was one thing, but our time together was something else. My side adventure to IKEA tonight proved that much. We'd had *fun*. I haven't seen him smile that much in a long while. More than once I thought he might actually hold my hand.

But this would only work if he met me halfway.

There must have been something in my expression that told him I wasn't screwing around. Gareth turned his face from me and let out a huff. "I trust you, Liz. More than I think you realize."

Well. Good. "Are you going to let me stay in charge? Because we can stop right now if you want."

"No." He rolled his head so his cheek rested on his biceps. "You're the boss, Mistress."

It really was impressive the power one little word held.

Rather than go back to his wrists, I bent down and freed his feet. I had to force my concentration back into the *being in charge Liz,* because it really wasn't my normal state. Not with Gareth at any rate. This time when I returned to work on his wrists, he didn't struggle, though he didn't do anything to help either.

I nearly forgot to take his arms down one at a time, making sure to give his shoulders and biceps a rub as I went. Even though he hadn't been up there for long, sometimes it didn't take much for that dull ache to set into your muscles.

Through the whole thing, Gareth said nothing. I kept sneaking glances at him, but his gaze was fixed somewhere on the floor. I knew that expression—I'd seen it enough in the mirror. The bastard was thinking again.

"I want you to lie faceup on the bed. Make sure you grab hold of my headboard and stretch out as far as you can."

Not for the first time I was thankful I'd purchased the wrought-iron frame when I'd first graduated from school. I intently watched as he climbed along the length of my mattress to stretch out onto his back. Tight muscles flexed as he shifted and adjusted into place. He still wasn't looking at me, which was beyond odd for him. Normally Gareth couldn't take his eyes off me.

No, that wasn't conceit.

I understood the appeal of simply being able to stare at an attractive naked body. There was something raw about it, as though you were able to see more than the bare flesh. I wanted to find a way to imprint myself on him, somewhere he'd never be able to get rid of. Maybe a place in his heart close to where his late wife was.

The leather and silk I wore had suddenly grown uncomfortable.

I'd often wondered why Gareth never bothered to dress up the way Stephen did. But now I understood. The clothing was only a mask. The real control, the place where the dominant part of him lived, didn't need the barrier to slip in and out of existence. It was a distraction from what was really important.

I sat down on the side of the bed and unzipped my boots. Okay, that felt a hundred times better. I placed them to the side before going to work on my corset. The muscles in Gareth's arms tensed and relaxed as I stripped, but he still wouldn't look at me. I didn't bother doing anything with the clothing, letting it fall to the floor in a silent heap.

My knees pressed into the bed, causing his body to shift as I got into position. I leaned over him and placed a kiss to his sternum.

"No matter what I do, don't let go of the headboard."

Oh, that got his internal hamster wheel spinning.

Gareth flexed his grip on the spindles and widened his legs. Still no words. God, we were going to have to work at this whole not talking thing.

"Gareth, how long have we known each other?"

Another tiny huff. "Two months."

"Hard to believe it's only been such a short time. I feel as if I've known you a lot longer."

He swallowed hard, but no other comment.

I shifted my knees so they pressed against his side. A sheen of sweat covered both of us now. I should get up and turn on the fan, or at least open the window. I wouldn't because either action would take me away from him.

Instead, I licked a slow path from one of his nipples to the other. "What did you think of me the first time you saw me?"

"That thank God you weren't some crazy woman. I also wondered why the hell had you spent so much on me at that auction."

That earned him a bite on the collarbone. "Smart-ass. I mean when you saw me in the crowd. When you were still standing behind the curtain."

When he didn't answer right away, I started to work my way down his body, nipping and licking every enticing bit of skin I saw. It wasn't until I reached the side of his stomach that he tried to squirm away.

"I thought you looked a bit lost. Stop that!"

"No, I'm in control and this is what I want to do." This time I licked across his belly button, pointedly ignoring his cock. "What do you mean I looked lost?"

Gareth bucked his hips. I shifted to lick down his thigh.

"Liz . . ."

"Gareth . . ."

"I mean, you looked as though you wanted what was being shown to you so badly, but you didn't have the first clue how to ask for it. You looked as if you were waiting for someone to take you by the hand and show you how good your body could feel. You wanted someone in your life who understood you."

Somewhere in his speech I'd stopped teasing him and simply looked. His face was flushed and his breathing had gone shallow and rapid. More importantly, he was looking at me.

Me.

I curled my fingers around the flesh of his leg. "Did you think . . ." I had to swallow. "Did you think you were the one? Who knew what I needed?"

He opened and closed his mouth a few times before nodding.

Now, I don't know if it was because of all the teasing, or if I simply didn't have the resolve to continue with the game anymore, but something in me simply broke. Without asking, I swung my leg over him and pressed my damp pussy to his stomach. I leaned my hands against his shoulders, forcing him to stay in place.

"Say it. Please, I really need you to say it." A tremor started deep inside me and for a moment I wasn't sure if it was from desire or emotion. Either way, I knew I was standing on the edge of something big.

I wanted to jump off the ledge, but I wouldn't unless he came with me.

Gareth lifted his head off the pillow, closing the already short distance between us. I didn't know where to look—his eyes, his mouth, the freckles that were only visible from close up. I found myself staring at his lips, wanting to be certain I understood the words when he actually spoke them.

"Yes." His tongue peeked out from behind his lips, teasing as he spoke. "When I first saw you, I thought I could be the one to show you. It was the first time I'd thought anything close to that in a long time."

My head spun.

He wanted me. He saw something inside of me that spoke to him.

I leaned in and sucked on his bottom lip as I pressed my cunt to his stomach. "Me?"

"Yes."

The tip of his cock brushed against my ass, proving to me that I wasn't the only one interested in this. It would be easy to shift backward and impale myself on him. I couldn't do that, though. He'd been holding out on me for a long time and I couldn't cross that line, abuse the trust he'd given me.

"Gareth, I want you. I want you to fuck me." I paused, wanting to give my words a moment to sink in. "Really, I want more than that, but for now I'll settle for riding your cock until we're both screaming and begging. Can I do that?"

No girl wants to hear *no* in the bedroom, any more than any man does. But in that moment I would have been okay with it, if only because I understood. He'd been stuck in a rut for so long, scared to move forward and leave the past behind, so having to deal with some crazy woman he'd just met at a charity auction wasn't the easiest thing to get one's head around.

But now I knew we were both starting to see things in the same light. We were slowly converging onto the same path and if the fates were smiling down on me, we'd have each other for the journey.

However, when Gareth groaned and nodded his consent, I was ready to jump out of bed and do an actual Snoopy dance.

"Condoms?" His voice shocked me out of my mental jubilation. And of course he was grinning. He knew exactly what I'd been doing. "We need condoms, Liz."

Right.

Safe sex.

I shoved my hand under my pillow, blindly searching for the strip I'd shoved there in my haste after Connie and Stephen had left. "I had them here somewhere. . . ."

He had to roll to the side and I had to lift up the pillow, but eventually I found them. Waving the strip of four in front of his nose, I grinned. "I had high hopes for tonight."

"I wouldn't expect anything less from you. Now, am I allowed to let go of this headboard?"

"Oh, hell no!" I gave his hands a slap on principle. "I'm still in control."

"Of course you are." He winked at me. He actually winked.

"You are such a smart-ass."

"It's called topping from below. You should be familiar with the concept."

"I'll show you topping—"

I pushed myself so his cock scraped along the outside of my bare pussy. I was quite wet at this point and his head came back shiny. Always the curious one, I leaned down and sucked his head into my mouth, enjoying the taste of my arousal on him. His cock pulsed against my tongue. He wouldn't be able to take much more of the teasing.

For once my hands were steady as I tore the condom package open. It had been a long time since I'd put one on a man. The lube was slick and made it a bit challenging to get the condom in place. Once I did, it was fun to roll it down the length of his shaft, teasing his balls when I hit the bottom.

"If you keep doing that, you're not going to get your ride."

Fuck that.

As soon as I grabbed the base of his shaft and lined myself up with his head, it suddenly became quite hard to breathe. This was it. After months of waiting, wondering, dreaming about it, I was finally going to get the one thing I wanted. I knew he was going to be amazing, because Gareth settled for nothing less. But what if he wasn't satisfied with me? What if I was a colossal letdown and that was why he'd been putting off—

"Liz! Breathe."

I sucked in a breath.

"It's going to be amazing. I want you so bad, baby. Fuck me. Please."

A part of me died a happy death.

I let my body lower, trying not to think of anything beyond the amazing sensations. Holy shit, he was so big. My muscles stretched to accommodate him, pulling him in as deep as I could take him. When my swollen clit brushed against his pubic hair, I nearly came undone.

I had to force myself not to move, taking several deep breaths so I wouldn't come on the spot. This was it. Gareth was inside me. The smell of his arousal mixed with mine filled the room. It was different from the times we'd played. That was only the smell of sex.

This was something different.

Shifting my feet so I had leverage, I placed my hands on his shoulders and began to slowly ride him. Before Gareth, anytime I'd had sex with a man, I'd always had to have direct stimulation to my clit to be able to get me off. Now, as I rode him, I could feel every inch of his thick cock against the insides of my cunt. The tingle that filled me ran hot through my body. My nipples hardened and my clit pulsed.

On every down thrust I would grind myself. Gareth groaned a few times and I could feel his body shaking. I knew if I said the word he would grab my hips, flip me over, and pound me into the mattress. That really did sound fucking fantastic. Maybe next time.

"Hands still." I slurred the last word as he slammed his hips up to meet mine, crushing my clit between us. "Do that again."

Okay, so I could compromise.

Our rhythm started off steady. I made sure he was looking at me before I widened my legs and let my pussy slam against him with every thrust. There was something wonderful about seeing his eyes widen with every contact. The way his mouth would part and the saliva on his lips would dry, making the skin pucker.

It was weird, the way I was focused on all the tiny details. How his brown eyes seemed to change the more aroused he got. The irises looked golden, warm, as if a fire had been ignited somewhere deep inside him and only now was I able to see the blaze.

I was hyperaware of my body, too. The way sweat ran along the side of my breast, tickling the skin as it slipped beneath the mound. The way my nipples seemed to absorb the pleasure I felt every time my breasts swung forward. I wanted him to reach up and squeeze them, pinch my nipples, pull at them until I couldn't stand it anymore.

"Gareth—"

I don't know how he knew, but his hands were suddenly exactly where I wanted them. His palms were cold from the metal, sending a sharp twinge through the stiffened and sensitive peaks.

"Yes." I squeezed my eyes shut and ignored the easy beat we seemed to have slipped into. This was for me, as much as it was for him. I ground down on him, taking and taking every bit of desire and craving I'd had built up for him. Two months and a lifetime of longing for this special connection.

There it was. That pressure that seemed to tickle my clit from the inside out. The pins and needles sensations I'd get at the base of my spine when I was about to have a mind-blowing release. Harder I slammed myself down on him. Gareth caught my nipples between his fingers and squeezed.

The rush of pleasure didn't roll through in a lazy wave. This time it was as though I'd exploded from every cell in my body. Joy and satisfaction so powerful, I'd never experienced that intensity before. It ripped me apart. I couldn't see past the haze, couldn't think beyond *oh my God, oh my God* until my brain gave up and took whatever my body threw at it.

When my hearing returned, I realized that the buzz I was hearing was actually my voice. "More, more, more."

Gareth sat up and took me with him. My head was now pressed against the foot of my mattress and he spread my legs wide. Large, strong fingers were wrapped around my ankles, holding me open for him to take.

Finally take.

A single thrust and he was reseated back deep inside me. My clit, already sensitive from my orgasm, could barely handle the sensory overload as he fucked me hard. I wanted to keep my eyes open and watch him lose himself, but I was fast losing the will and the energy.

I settled for catching quick glances of his face on every thrust forward. He'd closed his eyes, so I couldn't see that burning anymore. But it didn't matter. His expression of unrepressed lust, joy, relief told me everything I needed to know.

"Liz," he whispered as he tightened his hold on my legs.

"Do it. Fuck me. Make me come again."

Gareth fell forward on me and curled his arms around my shoulders. I couldn't move, could barely breathe as he fucked into me so fast I could feel each thrust in my bones.

He bit down on my neck, dug his fingers into me, and cried out. I bucked my hips up, wanting to catch every ounce of his cum with my body. The change in angle and the strength of his body surprised me with a second orgasm.

God, this was it. I could die now.

Gareth finally stopped, though he didn't move off of me. I kept my eyes closed and enjoyed my victory. This was what I'd wanted, to be pressed beneath him, to feel protected and owned. His breath hot against my skin. Sweat rolling down my neck, tickling as it went. He licked at it and I couldn't help but giggle.

"I love you," I whispered against him.

If you were to ask me later, I would say that I'd never intended to say that at all, let alone after we'd finally had sex. I mean, I was certain I could fall in love with the right someone after such a short time, but there was no way he was ready for any declarations.

It really shouldn't have been as much of a surprise then when he pushed himself off me and rolled to the far side of the bed. It shouldn't have, but it did.

"What?" I don't think I ever remember seeing his eyes quite that wide before. "What did you say?"

Shit. "I'm sorry. It just came out. You know how things can be after great sex—"

"Book."

My entire world screeched to a halt. "What?"

He was up, searching for his clothing on the floor. "I have to go."

"You used your safeword." My throat tightened and I didn't think I could breathe, let alone cry. "Gareth?"

"I'm sorry, Liz. I need to . . . I'm sorry."

I couldn't find the energy to follow him. I hugged myself and listened as he got dressed and left.

So that was that. The first man I'd ever felt I had a real connection to in my life, and I scared him off with three little words.

I knew he wasn't scared to say them. He'd been in love, deeply, with his wife. Who the hell did I think I was that I could push my way into his life to try to take her place?

I was Liz. Silly little Liz, who thought she could reach out and take a small piece of something big and wonderful for herself.

Foolish Liz who ruined everything by not thinking.

I lay back on the mattress and tried to find the energy to cry.

CHAPTER 11

I'm not sure why I let Connie talk me into going back to the Tail Whip. There was no charity auction this time, and I couldn't claim ignorance as to what went on there. She and Stephen had disappeared early on in the evening, leaving me to nurse my drink and watch a Domme flog her sub before she fucked him in the ass with a strap-on.

At least someone was having a good night.

Music filled the air, giving the place a happy vibe. I'd discovered that the stage that had been present for the auction was an actual part of the club. The curtains had come down and a St. Andrew's Cross filled a good portion of the area. It was far more intimidating to see someone tied to it here in this public place than it was to see Stephen's.

The club wasn't really a bar. They normally only served soft drinks and mineral water. Right then I'd been enjoying the effervescent taste of soda water with cherry, not the rum and Coke I desperately wanted.

This was stupid. There was nothing for me here and the last thing I wanted was to try to find someone else to take me on another magical wonder ride through BDSM land. Connie would know I went home when she came looking for me. Hell, I would swing by the grocery store on my way and pick up a tub of ice cream. There had to be an action movie or bad horror film on TV tonight.

I'd swallowed down the last of my water when I felt a hand touch my shoulder. I don't know whom I'd been expecting to see, but the bleached-blond man with an eyebrow piercing and a tattoo on the side of his neck wasn't it.

"You waiting for someone?" His smirk was . . . interesting.

"I came here with friends, but I think they've gone off to the back room."

"You're sitting here looking all pretty." His hand slid up to cup the back of my head, his fingers tightening in my hair. "A pretty-looking sub waiting for a good time. I'll take you out back and show you one."

"Thanks, but I'm not interested."

In all fairness to blond boy, as soon as I said no, he let my hair go. I knew that despite the attitude, he wasn't going to play if all parties weren't happy with the arrangement. So, when I blinked and realized that Gareth was standing directly behind him, I didn't think anything of it.

Well, my brain hadn't caught up to things.

I mean, it didn't seem wrong for Gareth to be there. For a moment I'd forgotten that I hadn't spoken to him in nearly three weeks. But then I realized he was wearing his glasses, not his contacts. He wasn't here for a scene.

"Let her go." His voice was so low I could feel the base of it rumble through me. Or maybe that was simply my reaction to him.

Shit, he was here for me.

Blond boy lifted his hand from my back and took a step away. "The lady said she wasn't interested. I was about to walk away."

"You better move your ass. If I see you even looking at my girl again, I'll fuck you up so hard you'll wish I'd killed you."

I'd frozen in my spot on the stool, blond boy completely forgotten as Gareth stepped into view. *My girl?* He hadn't said a word to me since that night, hadn't bothered to even talk to Stephen to see how I was doing. If I'd been crying over him? Hell, if I'd managed to *stop* crying once the floodgates had opened?

"My girl?" I slipped from the stool, grabbing my purse.

"Liz."

"Fuck you."

I walked past the stage where the Domme was helping her man from the spanking bench she'd placed him on. His ass was a beautiful red and his face was streaked with tears. Those were the good kind, the ones brought out by reaching a spot so deep inside your head all the dark and nasty stuff inside you bled out.

I hadn't felt that in a while.

"Liz!"

If I stopped and looked at him, I knew I wouldn't have the strength to make a clean break. He wasn't in love with me—fine. But if I allowed myself to continue to see him, knowing my feelings weren't going to be reciprocated, that made me a fool. I am many things, but not that.

"Liz, will you stop and listen to me?"

"No, go away."

Stephen had driven us to the club, which meant I either had to walk, find a taxi, or take the subway. The next stop was at least two blocks away. Gareth didn't look as though he was about to let me go.

"I need to talk to you."

"Too bad." A taxi was my best bet. Though there's never one when you need it.

Gareth caught my arm and tugged at me to stop. When I whirled around and punched him hard on the chest, he staggered back, holding his hands up.

"I'm sorry, but I really need to talk to you."

God, he looked shitty, as if he hadn't slept in a month. Well, good. I'd hate to think I was the only one suffering through all this.

"I don't think there is anything left to say." Pushing my hair from my eyes, I caught a glimpse of a taxi coming toward us. "I'm going home."

"At least let me drive you. I promise that once I know you're home safe I'll leave you alone. I won't chase you into the apartment or anything."

The drive wouldn't take more than twenty minutes this late at night. There was next to no traffic on the streets. But I wasn't sure if I could handle being in the same building as him, let alone the confines of a car for that long. Indecision had always been my enemy and the taxi drove past before I could make my body move to stop it.

"Please, baby." Gareth reached forward and took my hand again, this time far gentler than before. "I promise to behave."

My mouth had grown dry and my hands were starting to moisten. I tugged my hand away and simply nodded. I don't think I could have said anything.

"Thank you. I'm parked just down here."

We walked in silence to his car. I wanted to believe that I wasn't affected by the simple presence of a man, or the scent of aftershave. I've been my own woman since I moved from home and had been proud of what I've accomplished since then.

But my body remembered what Gareth had done to me. My traitorous skin prickled at the memory of his hands on it, the bite and sting in the muscles as he'd land spanks against my ass. My pussy clenched, longing to feel his cock press back into my core once more.

I stopped at the sight of his car. I couldn't do this and come out the other end whole. "I'm going to wait for a cab."

"Liz." Gareth pinched the bridge of his nose. His shoulders tensed as he turned to face me. "I didn't want to do this in public, but I will."

"Do what?" I knew there was only a short list of things he wouldn't do.

"This."

My body wouldn't move as he took the three steps to close the distance between us. I'd forgotten how much taller he was than me, how much I loved the look of his unshaven face. Gareth leaned down, slow enough to project what he was about to do. His mouth brushed against mine, setting the skin on fire.

"I've missed you and I'm sorry." His whispered words were punctuated with a light kiss. "I hate myself for what I did to you."

"Why?" *Why did you do it? Why did you leave? Why in hell are we standing here at one in the morning?*

"You were right. I'd been hiding. I was scared if I moved on that it would be as if I didn't love Rachael anymore. As if I'd never really loved her at all."

I pulled my head back but didn't move away.

Gareth closed his eyes. "The two of you would have gotten along famously. She was so much fun, loved to tease me, tease anyone. One minute she was there laughing at me, and the next they told me she was gone."

Oh.

Oh my God.

I'd been completely oblivious to the fact that he'd still been grieving. I thought he'd simply been too scared to move on. How the hell could I have been so blind to something so important? That I'd misunderstood his emotions all this time? Shit, I was such an asshole. "I'm sorry."

"You have no reason to be." He kissed my forehead, before moving away. "Do you mind if we take this to the car?"

The night air was growing chilly, but that wasn't what had me agreeing and following him. Gareth opened the passenger door for me and stepped back to let me in. One look at him and I knew that wasn't going to work. I reached past him and opened the back door, sliding across the seat to the far side.

"What are you doing?" He leaned in and frowned at me.

"Just come back here so we can talk."

The moment the door shut, I felt the change in the air. Gareth took up a generous part of the back, his head nearly touching the ceiling. I'd forgotten how much I enjoyed being next to him.

Dammit, I still loved him.

He looked over at me and placed his hand on my leg. "This okay?"

"Yeah. Look, I'm the one who should be sorry. I didn't give any thought to your feelings. I certainly shouldn't have said what I did, heat of the moment or not."

Gareth pushed his glasses up his nose as he struggled to speak. Finally he took them off and placed them behind him by the window. "I've been angry for a long time. When Rachael was first killed, I spent more time drunk than sober. She would have been so pissed if she'd seen me that way."

"Is that why you stopped?"

"No, I'd ended up in the hospital after falling down the stairs. I was lucky not to have broken my neck. After that I knew I had to put the bottle down and smarten up. I swore that if I couldn't have her, then I'd do everything in my power to stay true to her."

"You must have loved her very much." I couldn't imagine giving that kind of devotion to someone, let alone be on the receiving end.

God, I was such a liar. The three weeks since he'd walked out had shown me that if nothing else, Gareth would always have a piece of my heart, even if I didn't have his.

"She was the first woman who encouraged my Dom tendencies in the bedroom. She'd read up on positions, techniques, encouraged me to try things. She wasn't afraid of anything."

I imagined it was the same as being in love for the first time. That rush you feel at first when everything is new, sexy, wild. "How long had you two been together?"

"Four years, but we'd only gotten hardcore into BDSM for the last year."

Gareth's hand had tightened on my knee. I couldn't tell if he was trying to ground himself in the present, or if he was scared I was going to run away on him.

Regardless, I placed my hand over his and squeezed back. "So, that auction?"

"Was my way of trying to get back into the land of the living. Stephen said it would be the perfect thing to try, meet someone and there'd be no strings attached. It would give me a chance to see if I really was a Dom, or if I'd only been that way with Rache."

"So, when I chased you down at the university, that was unexpected."

"Unexpected, but not unwelcomed." Gareth turned to face me more, picking my hand up in his. "When you were standing there after my class, I wasn't sure if I was more scared that you being there was a beginning or an end. I'd only just admitted to myself that I was lonely."

He lifted my hand to his lips and kissed each of my knuckles. "I tried to fool myself into thinking that if I kept things being only about you, that I wasn't betraying Rachael and I could still have something new for myself. But every time we got together, I saw in your eyes that it wasn't enough."

"I didn't want to push you. You told me that you didn't want a relationship and I was trying to respect that. Every time I wanted more, I tried to squash that feeling down. Until I couldn't. I didn't want to hurt you. Did I? Hurt you?"

"No, but I knew you wanted more from me. I wasn't sure I could give it to you. In my head it felt as though I was going to have to say good-bye to her. I didn't know if I could do that."

"I would never ask you to."

"I realize that now. But when you said you loved me . . . I thought that was it. I had to make a decision and choose between you."

I leaned in and kissed him hard. His tongue met mine, pushing and sliding against each other in an intimate caress. Stubble rubbed against my chin and cheek, keeping me focused solely on him. On us. "I want you." I moved to bite at his earlobe. "If you're saying good-bye, wait until after because I really need to fuck you now."

Gareth took my face in his hands and pulled me back. "That's what

I've been trying to tell you. These past three weeks nearly killed me. It hurt almost as much as when I lost Rache, except this time it was my fault. I couldn't do that to either of us."

Oh. "So, you don't hate me?"

He chuckled and nipped at the end of my nose. "How the hell could anyone hate you?"

"You'd be surprised. There are at least three people at work."

"Well, they're morons." Gareth looked straight into my eyes and smiled. "I wanted to tell you that I'm not sure how you managed to work your way into my heart so fast, but I love you, Liz."

"You . . ." I was grinning like a fool.

"Love you. Yes." He kissed me hard enough to make my head spin. "Now get on your knees and suck my cock."

It's impossible to drop to one's knees in the backseat of a car with any bit of grace. Given the length of Gareth's body, it was challenging to move myself between his thighs and still have enough room to get his jeans down. Working together, we managed to get one shoe and one leg free, making it far easier to yank down his briefs.

The car was instantly filled with the scent of sex. Fuck, I was about to give him a blow job in the back of a car on the side of a street. It didn't matter that it was one in the morning and cops could be by at any time. Hell, *anyone* could be by to see what we were doing.

I opened wide and sucked him down as far as I could in one go. Gareth's fingers found my head and I recognized that instant urge for him to control the situation. He pulled my hair up, bunching it into one fist so he could direct the speed of my bobbing. Free from the tickle of the strands, I trusted him to pay enough attention to the world around us so we wouldn't get arrested, closed my eyes, and went to work.

My tongue pressed along the underside of his cock, teasing the sensitive spot I knew was there. I let my teeth scrape against his skin, upping the pain threshold a bit more. He might enjoy being in charge, but I now knew he didn't mind a bit of bite with his pleasure.

"This is how I've been picturing you for weeks." He placed a hand on my shoulder and squeezed my hair. "Every time I'd close my eyes I'd see you down there, sucking my cock, a look of bliss on your face. I love how much you let yourself go and enjoy the feeling of the moment."

God, I wanted to reach down and play with my clit, get myself to the edge until he told me I could come. I might not even need that, the sound of his voice, the barely restrained lust enough to push me over the edge.

"I wanted to come back so many times since I left. I wanted to tie you up to that bloody cross and spank your ass until you understood. I never let anyone do that to me before. Not even Rachael. She always needed me to take charge."

My mind was already cataloging things I wanted to do to him the next time I got to take over in the bedroom.

Gareth's cock pulsed in my mouth as he bucked up. If I placed my hands on his thighs and pushed myself up a bit, he'd have room to be able to fuck my face. It wouldn't take much to get him to—

"Liz, stop thinking." He reached down and pinched my nipple.

Right. No thinking.

He gently pulled me off his cock, ignoring my whimper. I don't think I could ever get tired of sucking him.

"Are you wearing any panties under that skirt?" There was a rough quality to his voice, something I hadn't heard before. Something primal.

"Yes." I could barely manage more than a whisper.

"Off. Now."

I'd never moved that fast before in my life. Instead of tossing my panties aside, Gareth took them and draped them over his glasses. "You won't be getting those back."

"No?"

"I'm still deciding if I want you wearing panties ever again. I'll let you know."

"Thank you, Sir."

"You're going to kill me, Liz." He gave the side of my neck a squeeze. "There's a condom in my pocket. Take it out and put it on me."

I'd been glad I'd already done this at least once to him, because this time my hands were shaking madly. We were in public fucking in the back of a car. The real threat of getting caught was a turn-on I'd never guessed it would be. Apparently, I was a closet exhibitionist. Maybe I would be able to get up on the cross back at the club. Once I had the latex on him, I spread the lube that clung to my fingers across my pussy.

"You have no idea how beautiful you are when you're turned on. Come here."

Without any sort of grace or ease, he pulled me up until I was able to straddle him. It was as though we knew our time was limited, that this cocoon we'd spun around us would break and the real world would invade. I didn't care—nothing would stop me from taking what I wanted.

And I wanted Gareth. Dominant, broken, beautiful Gareth.

Unlike the first time we'd done this, there was no hesitation in my moves. I lined myself up with him and sunk down hard on his cock. His hands found their way to my hips as he helped me find the leverage we both wanted. Fuck, there would be finger marks in my skin tomorrow from the strength of his grasp. I leaned in and sucked his earlobe into my mouth, nibbling at the sensitive skin with my teeth.

"That's it, Liz. Your cunt is so wet and eager. You've wanted me to fuck you for a long time. Not that shit we did the first time. You wanted me to take charge, give you what I wanted. Be careful what you wish for, Lizzy."

Gareth shoved one hand between us and pinched the outside top of my clit. The little bolt of pain had my pussy clamping down on his cock, forcing him even deeper. When he'd release the flesh a rush of pleasure would spark from the spot. Over and over he'd pinch and release, as he'd whisper in my ear.

"When I get you home, I'm going to cane your ass until it's red. I'm going to bind your body with rope. You won't be able to get away from me and what I do to you. I'm going to fuck your ass while I push a dildo into your cunt. I'll make you scream yourself raw."

I wrapped my arms around his head and pushed his face against the side of my throat. He spanked my ass hard three times as I drew closer to my orgasm. The momentum, the pain, being pressed so close to him, was all too much for me to handle. I sucked in a breath and bit down on his shoulder.

"Fuck, Liz." He leaned as far back as the seat would allow.

With my orgasm still rolling through me, I wanted to chase the pleasure, pull as much as I could from it. I rolled my hips, grinding down hard on him. It was enough to push him over. He didn't hold back his cries. The shout bounced off the widows, echoing back to me as another surge of pleasure erupted. I'm not sure how long we stayed cuddled together, shaking as we came down from our pleasure, but it was long enough for the widows to fog.

Gareth shifted me around so my head was resting comfortably against his shoulder and my legs were draped across his lap. He ran his fingers through my hair, wrapping strands around his fingers.

"Liz?"

"Hmm?"

"What you said to me the last time we did this?"

Nerves soured my stomach. "Yeah?"

"Do you still feel that way?"

I wasn't sure what answer he was looking for, but given his earlier reaction, I didn't think it was an escape route. "Do I think I love you?"

He nodded.

"Yeah, of course I do."

"Say it again."

"I love you, Gareth."

He lifted a strand of hair to his nose and breathed in the scent. "I'm really screwed up. You know that, right?"

"No more than I am."

"Maybe that means we'll be able to make a go of this."

I slipped my hand beneath his shirt and played with his chest hair. "Gareth?"

"Hmm?"

"Do you really think Rachael would have liked me?"

He pushed his fingers into my hair, before taking a strand and wrapping it around his finger. "She would have loved you. In fact, I bet she would be happy knowing we were together."

"Really?" It's weird hoping to have the approval of someone who's died.

"Really. And she'd expect that I'd treat you like a princess, unless you've been a bad, bad girl."

Looking up into his beautiful brown eyes, I couldn't stop myself from grinning. "Then I better learn to behave."

"I hope not, baby. I hope not."

PART 3

SEDUCING THE SUBMISSIVE

CHAPTER 12

I'd always assumed that when you fall in love with someone, then you've pretty much secured your happily ever after. Right? I mean, that's where all the books and movies leave the hero and heroine once they've fought off all the bad guys and monsters and stuff. They'd earned the right to be happy.

I'd thought Gareth and I had earned that right, too.

Four months, that's how long we'd been a couple, and I've loved every second of it. It seemed I couldn't go more than a few minutes without thinking about him. Even when I should be concentrating on my lunch and the meeting I had after, I couldn't do it. How could I when I'd spent most of my lunch hour coming up with the best surprise for him? I crossed my legs and nudged the bag under the table with my shoe.

Besides, thinking about Gareth was far better than the alternative.

Work had been a horrible place for the past month, and I did everything I could to mentally distance myself. I'd even shifted my lunch break to later in the day so I wouldn't have to listen to all the rampant speculation and negativity about what had happened. The lunch room wasn't that big, so it wasn't like there was a corner I could go hide in. Not to mention I had quite a few work friends here who loved to chat whenever the opportunity arose. These days there was only the one topic. I'd spent the last two years working at Schultz Associates as a community outreach specialist. It was pretty much my professional dream job come true. I got to work with charities on special events, getting them corporate dollars and prize donations to assist in their causes. I felt great about what I did, and the company had an awesome corporate image.

That was until our VP of Sales, Simon Caldwell, got arrested. Internally, management hadn't said much to us other than: *They were aware of the situation and would let the courts and due process handle matters* . . . blah blah blah. They didn't have a clue about what to say or how to react. So everything stayed quiet until we got some details.

Oh boy, did we ever get details.

It's amazing how fast the phone stops ringing when a prominent player in your company is accused of sexual assault of multiple women.

Caldwell had claimed that everything had been a misunderstanding. He was into BDSM and this was nothing more than his love of rough sex. The women who'd accused him knew upfront what he liked. Experts were brought on the newscasts to discuss the case, the psychology behind kink. . . .

It was a lot to take in.

I'd tried to talk to Gareth about it a bit when the story first broke, but he grew quiet and refused to get into it. We kept doing our thing, but I couldn't stop my brain from latching on to what was being said.

Connie suggested I get my mind off things by going shopping. The plain gray bag hiding on the floor by my feet held a new flogger that I was hoping I could convince Gareth to use on me tomorrow night. Not that it would take much in the way of convincing. My trip to the sex store had taken me a bit longer than I'd anticipated, which left me only a few minutes to scarf down my leftover chicken and rice from the restaurant Gareth had taken me to a few nights earlier. He'd flirted with me the entire night, teasing me about what he was going to do when we got back to his place. We hadn't finished our meal in our rush to get out of there, hence my leftovers.

I wanted to focus on my lunch, because damn this stuff was awesome, but I couldn't. No, my head was in the gutter picturing how things would go when I showed Gareth my gift for him.

With every bite I let my imagination run, knowing just how his eyes would gleam when I handed him the flogger. The way he'd try to keep his face devoid of emotion, but would fail and smirk as I would beg him to use it on me. The way his eyes would light up when I'd slip in a soft *Sir* and drop slowly to my knees.

Oh yeah. It was going to be a good night.

I was lost in a particularly wonderful mental picture when three ladies from the accounting department came in and took up residence at one of the empty tables near me. They were all named Donna, which was weird in itself. Normally, it took little effort to ignore their magpie chatter. Numbers, accounts, and approvals wasn't my thing. But with one sentence, they grabbed my attention in an iron grasp.

"I think anyone who lets a man tie them up in the bedroom is a freak."

My mouth fell open and my fork stopped halfway to my lips. When I regained my composure, I shoved my food into my mouth and swallowed without tasting. I peeked down at the bag containing my purchase and pushed it a bit deeper beneath the table.

Donna One slammed the microwave door shut. "I'm sorry, getting tied up and beaten is abuse. Any idiot should know that."

"Yeah, but you don't know what he said to them to get them in there. I mean, they're saying he was abusive, but only after they'd agreed to have sex. He choked one woman until she almost passed out." Donna Two took a sandwich out of her lunch bag. "You met Caldwell. Dude was hot. I can see why women would go out with him, but not let him do shit like that."

Donna Three was a reed-thin woman who never seemed to eat. She slugged back her coffee. "Kinky sex with him would be interesting. You've read those books. And I'm pretty sure you like them." She giggled. I did my best not to roll my eyes. Gareth read one page of one of Connie's favorite erotic books and threw it in the garbage. *That's where it belongs.*

Personally, I kind of liked them.

Donna One snorted. "No, that was abuse. It's all wrong. There've been studies done on this stuff. People who are into that BDSM have been abused as kids. They don't know any better."

Donna Two shook her sandwich at Donna One. "I don't buy that. They can't all be abused. And I know of people who don't like sex at all because of childhood trauma."

Donna One crossed her arms and stared at her friend. "Fine, I wasn't sure on that one either. Still, can you imagine what kind of person wants that kind of relationship? Low self-esteem or some such shit. Can't make their own decisions so they hook up with a guy who gets off on telling them what to do. I don't know. It's certainly not normal. I don't understand it. I never did."

Donna Three tossed her empty coffee cup into the garbage can. "It's not the people who get off on the pain that you need to worry about. That's their business. It's the sick bastards like Caldwell who are the problem. They're beating those poor women. I mean, it shouldn't matter what the women liked. If he went too far, then it was too far. End of story."

At some point during their tirade, I'd lost my appetite. The Donnas continued to talk about Caldwell and the women, but I wasn't listening.

Am I like that? Is Gareth?

Sure, I wasn't the type to take charge of a situation. Even when I'd spent the night with Gareth and took over for his little training session, it wasn't natural for me. Not that I'd minded it, but I took far more pleasure when he was the one with the flogger in hand.

Was there something wrong with me for enjoying what we did together?

I'd never questioned it before. Yeah, I knew it wasn't everyone's thing, but after having spent some time at the Tail Whip and seeing firsthand Connie and Stephen's relationship, the whole lifestyle didn't seem weird to me. They loved each other. Hell, they'd finally set their wedding date and were already talking about having kids. You couldn't get any more normal than that.

And the idea that Gareth might be a sociopath? Or Stephen? No way.

I packed up my lunch and tried to shove my purchase in my lunch bag before getting up to leave. Of course it didn't fit.

"Hey, Liz! It's Liz, right?" Donna Three waved at me.

Fuck.

I smiled and pulled my lunch bag a bit closer to my body. "Hey."

Donna Three smiled. "What do you think about the Caldwell thing?"

You really don't want to know. "I don't know. I'm sure we'll get more information from management."

Donna Two snorted. "Yeah right. They didn't even tell us before they had layoffs two years ago. I found out in the news right after they let part of the team go."

"I can tell you this," Donna One said as she dug into her lunch. "They'll be keeping a closer eye on all of us. God help anyone who is looking for a promotion. Justin in HR told me that they have him on social media duty."

My stomach turned and a tremor raced through me. "Pardon?"

"Yeah, they have him checking out Facebook and Instagram and stuff for anyone who they're hiring. He said they can't afford to have another PR fight on top of this one, so if anyone has anything even remotely off-color posted, it will be an instant black mark."

"I applied for a team lead role last month." Oh, shit. I wanted to puke. I didn't have anything bad on my Facebook page, did I? God, I couldn't even remember what groups I was a part of anymore.

The trio giggled.

"You might want to go home and check that out. Though you don't strike me as a person who'd post drunken nudes or weird sex stuff." Donna One winked at me.

Double fuck.

"What's in the bag?" Donna Three piped up. "Did you go shopping? God, I've been meaning to head across the street and check out the sale at The Bay."

And I was out of there. "Sorry, ladies, I have to get back."

I didn't bother to wait for them to say anything else before I bolted from the lunch room. The hidden flogger became a giant screaming siren in my mind. Why the hell did I have to go out and buy something like this and bring it into the office? Though I didn't have a car to leave it in, and sure no one could see it, but the fact that I had a sex toy in the office, a place where one of the VPs had been accused of sex crimes . . .

Stupid idiot!

Looking around to make sure no one was close, I took the bag with the flogger out and shoved it into my purse. Oh good, that worked. To make double sure no one would see it, I positioned my wallet above it before zipping my purse closed. I then shoved my purse into the bottom drawer of my filing cabinet.

It was only then that I was able to breathe.

The next order of business—double-checking my social media accounts. Not that I had put anything to do with BDSM online, but God only knew how sensitive the company would be about things.

The fact that they had Justin checking online presences was enough to freak me out.

This was crazy. When had life gotten so tense? Things were supposed to be better now that Gareth and I had found one another.

Right then, I wanted nothing more than to call him, see him, wrap myself in his arms and let him distract me. We weren't planning on getting together until tomorrow night, but I didn't think I could wait that long. Not after everything that had been going on today.

Perhaps it was time for me to pay the professor a visit. He could use more surprises in his life. And I have a wonderful present to give him. With a smile fixed on my face, I checked the bus schedule and worked out the details to check in on Gareth.

This would be fun.

CHAPTER 13

I still got that familiar rush of awkwardness when I showed up to visit Gareth at his school. You'd think that I'd be used to walking the halls of the old brick building by now, but I couldn't help but feel out of place. It had been more than a few years since I'd graduated from my own business program, and I couldn't get over how old I felt compared to the current mix of students.

I wasn't all that old, but these guys were babies! They looked as though they were twelve or something.

It had been awhile since I'd showed up during one of his classes. This was a new semester for him, but he'd mentioned that he was teaching third-year students this time around. I knew how much the freshmen drove him nuts last term, so I was happy that he had the change this time around—though I would miss some of our role-playing discipline sessions that we'd done to help alleviate his stress, when Master Gareth turned into Professor Gareth and I'd *forgotten* to hand in an assignment.

The spankings . . .

The begging . . .

My pussy dampened at that particular memory. He'd broken out a new paddle that night, one that I'd insisted we use many times since.

I knew the building and floor where he taught, but not the specific room. Not that it mattered. No one else sounded quite like him, which meant it would be easy enough for me to hunt him down. Gareth's voice had a rich quality to it, one that sent a chill down my spine every time I heard him. Closing my eyes, I listened to the sounds echoing down the hallway. The muted murmur of voices seeped through closed doors. I walked a few paces, my fingers against the cold brick wall to guide me as I located him.

There.

His voice was coming from a room just up and to the left. Even with the door closed I knew Gareth was on the other side. I could tell that he was excited about whatever it was he was saying. His voice had grown louder and he was speaking in a rush. I'd never ever tell him, but I loved seeing this side of his personality. When he was with me, Gareth was still pretty reserved. And when we started playing, Master Gareth was anything but a light and fluffy guy. His Dom persona was calm and collected. Everything was done with precision, every detail thought out and all angles considered. He was in control—of the situation, of the sex, of me—and I'd always loved that.

But here, when he was teaching, I was able to see a side of him that rarely came out at home. He was passionate about his subject, about literature and the history of the classics. Peeking in the window centered in the door to the classroom, I saw Gareth pacing in front of a table, a blank white board behind him. He had a book in his hand, but he wasn't looking at it. Instead, his focus was on his students as he lectured them about something. I wasn't much of a reader, but even I couldn't help but get drawn in to his enthusiasm.

I was still watching when he turned to pace back toward the door, and our gazes met. He stopped midsentence and his back straightened. Before I could see him react further, I turned and pressed my back to the wall. Shit, he was going to be pissed that I'd distracted him. Well, maybe not pissed, but he wouldn't be happy.

Again, not necessarily a bad thing for me.

I grinned and tried to stop from giggling.

Unfortunately for me, his class didn't end for another ten minutes, which gave me plenty of time to think. Each second I waited, I slid from excited to impatient and landed squarely in the land of anxious. Gareth wouldn't be upset with me showing up unexpectedly, would he? There was a time when we'd both use this as a pretext for a *punishment*. Any other day of the week I wouldn't have thought twice about what that meant. I wouldn't care about what people thought.

Today wasn't just any day.

I no longer knew what to think.

The door opened and a rush of students poured through into the hallway. Like the last semester, there were an abnormally high number of female students taking Gareth's class. And why the hell wouldn't there be? I remember signing up for a philosophy class because Professor Rosenberg was hot. That man had no business being in academia. As a student I would have been all over Gareth's course. I might have failed due to lack of attention to the subject matter, but I certainly would have had perfect attendance.

"Are you going to keep hiding out there or come say hello?"

My pussy dampened and a tingle zipped through me at the sound of his voice. Rolling my body against the wall, I stuck my head around the wall. "Sorry about that."

Gareth was sitting on his desk, his hands braced on either side of his body. "It's fine."

His gaze dropped to the spot in front of him for half a second before he met mine again. That was my cue to get my ass in there. Rather than jump to action like I normally would, I took a deep breath. "I can come back if you have another class."

"Last one of the day."

"Or some marking."

"That's why I hire a grad student."

"Or if you have a meeting—"

"Liz." Gareth gave his head a little shake, a smile playing on his lips. "Come here."

It was one thing to ignore a silent command. It was simply plain rude to ignore a request. Doing my best to ignore my heavy feet, I sauntered into the room.

We'd been together long enough now that I knew he could tell there was something wrong. Not that I'm a spectacular actress or anything. Standing in front of him, the scent of his cologne hit me and my muscles relaxed. I forced my gaze to meet his once again. He was wearing his contact lenses, which I loved. It made it easier to see the brown of his eyes. Unlike myself, Gareth was better at keeping his emotions under wraps. It caught me off guard when I looked at him and saw the concern reflected there.

"Are you okay?"

If I'd learned anything about Gareth since we'd gotten together, it was that there was no point in me trying to lie to him. First, I sucked at it. Second, he always knew. And whenever I tried to tell him that it was no big deal, he'd start to press. Far easier just to lay everything out there.

"Some women at the office were talking about Caldwell at lunch. Put me in a mood." There, the truth, even if it was an understatement.

"I see." Gareth looked away as he took my hands in his. "Dare I ask what they were saying?"

"Oh, you know. Women who are into that are freaks, or abused. Men who do it are crazy assholes. The usual."

"Ah."

"It just put me in a bad mood. Oh, and I found out that because of the PR fallout, anyone who is applying for a job in the company is having their social media scrutinized."

Gareth winced. "You applied for a job last month, right?"

"I went through my Facebook and stuff on my phone after work. There were a few pictures from the club, but they were tame." Women in corsets shouldn't spark any moral outrage, right? "I took them down just to be safe. Though at this point it might not matter."

"It's too bad you have to do that. I have no doubt that it will be fine. You said your boss had already put in a good word for you."

"He did." Internally, I was the best person qualified for the team lead role, but there was nothing stopping them from looking outside of the company either.

"Your work quality speaks for itself. It will work out." He leaned in and kissed my forehead.

"Thanks. I'm sorry to have bothered you here." I totally wasn't sorry.

"Sure you are." Gareth lifted my hands to his mouth and placed a kiss to the back of each one. "I know when you want some extra Gareth time. Come with me."

He didn't let go of my hand as he led me down the hall and around the corner. We stopped beside the vending machine and Gareth fished a key from his pocket.

Oh.

This was his office.

"Did you need to get something? I can wait out in the car if you're ready to—"

The rest of whatever I was going to say evaporated from my mind.

Gareth lowered his chin and narrowed his eyes. "Liz. Go into my office. Now."

If you'd told me a year ago that I'd follow a man's directive without so much as a second thought, I would have laughed at you. Full-blown giggle mode. And yet that look had become so familiar as his signal for *we are about to engage in a round of joyous, kinky fucking* that I couldn't bring up so much as a snicker. The second I complied there would be hot, messy sex.

In his office.

Fuck yeah.

I stepped in and did my best to steady my breathing. It was a trick that Connie had shown me over the past few months, a way to calm my body and find that spot in my brain that let me enjoy what we were about to do. If I didn't, it took me a long time to calm the whirlwind that blew around my head. Without being told to, I moved into the middle of his small office, dropped my purse to the floor, and closed my eyes.

Pulling a long breath in through my nose and out through my mouth, I focused on the sound of my beating heart. It was hard to concentrate on the steady, comforting thudding in my chest when Gareth—Master Gareth—was moving around me. I became aware of him picking up my purse, the click of the door being locked, the soft rustle of his pants as he shifted what sounded like papers and books, the dull thud and slide of a body on wood.

"Liz, open your eyes."

The moment I complied I was greeted with the sight of Master Gareth sitting on his desk. He'd removed his tie and unbuttoned his shirt, exposing the upper part of his chest. My gaze dipped down to his hand where he held a ruler. It was one of those old wooden ones, the black ink of the numbers looking faded.

Oh, this was going to be fun.

"You interrupted my class." There was no malice in his voice. No hint that he was actually angry with me for showing up. I wanted nothing more than to meet his gaze, make sure that the little spark that I loved seeing was present in his eyes. But that would be against the rules.

"I'm sorry, Sir." I still wasn't sorry.

"It might be easier to believe you if you weren't smirking."

I did my best to school my face. "I'll try harder, Sir."

"Come here."

A rush of desire bolted through me. My nipples tightened and I wanted to squeeze my thighs together to increase the rising pleasure. Walking the few steps across the office to where he stood was wonderfully arousing. I knew what was going to come next; still, I waited until he gave me the command.

"Take your shirt off."

My fingers no longer shook when I got undressed in front of him. I'd recognized this part of the game for what it was, my way to tease and seduce him. Rather than simply pull my shirt off over my head, I tucked my arms in through their respective holes and slowly lifted it up over my head. I made sure to stretch my arms up high, letting my body lengthen and my breasts thrust forward. I then folded my shirt and handed it to him.

God, I really wanted to look him in the eyes. Though the bulge in the front of his pants told me that my little show was appreciated.

"Now the bra."

I sucked in a breath, letting my breasts thrust forward as I reached behind me and released the clasp. The air in the office wasn't cold, but that didn't prevent my nipples from tightening more as they were finally exposed. I held out my bra for Master Gareth to take.

There was a slight pause before he took it from me. "Step closer." No compliments today. He must really be turned on.

Inching even closer than before, I managed not to flinch when he reached out and took my left breast in his hand. His forefinger and thumb found their way to my nipple, squeezing and rolling the tip until it was painfully erect. It was hard not to squirm, to roll my hips in such a way as to entice him to take things to the next step. That certainly wouldn't turn out my way.

"I don't have any of my normal toys here. I'll have to bring a few in case you decide you want to pay me any future visits." He pinged my nipple with his finger. I gasped and had to bite back a moan. "I'll have to improvise."

Not that I would ever tell him when we were playing, but I loved it when he improvised. It took Master Gareth outside of his normal routine, forced him to be even more creative than usual. So, when he looked around his desk and picked up a large, thick elastic band, my heart did a little leap.

"As a respectable member of the staff, it's important to lead by example. Just the other day I was talking to my students about the need to reuse items whenever possible. To find ways to repurpose them as necessary. This would make an excellent nipple clamp."

Oh. My. "Yes, Sir."

You'd think it would be easy to stand there and let someone wrap elastic around a part of you. I mean, I'd handled clamps and chains to this point, how bad could this be. Well, now I knew the answer to that because holy crap! With each twist of the band around my skin, the pinch grew exponentially. The tip went from red to purple, much the same way it did when I had the clamps on. This wasn't painful so much as it was intense. My body shivered from the unexpected on-slaught of sensations.

Master Gareth ran his thumb across the exposed part of my nipples. I could barely feel the brush of his skin against mine.

"So beautiful." He placed a kiss between my breasts. "I want you to suck me."

I was on my knees so fast I felt the vibrations up through my lower back. "Oh yes, Sir."

It was easy for me to free his hard cock from his pants. The smell of his arousal had my mouth watering and the pressure around my nipples sent waves of pleasure through my body.

"I don't want you to use your hands, just your mouth."

Of course he'd have to make it challenging.

Shifting my body farther between his thighs, I rose up as high as I could on my knees and ran my tongue up the length of his shaft. He tasted of sweat and desire. Some of his pubic hairs caught on my tongue as I continued to lick up his length like a treat. They tickled and caught, but I ignored them as best I could and shifted my attention to his head.

I knew how to play his body as well as he knew what I liked. If I licked the nerve bundle just so, the muscles in his thighs would begin to quiver. While I might not be allowed to use my hands, I could certainly use my chin to put the right amount of pressure on his balls.

And there was the bitten-off moan I'd wanted.

The most challenging part of all this was trying not to grin.

"You're having too much fun down there." His hands found their way to my hair, pulling me up and back at an awkward angle. "This is a punishment."

"Sorry, Sir."

"You always say that. I never believe you."

"I know." I didn't stop the smile from coming that time.

He tugged on my hair, encouraging me to rise to my feet. "I think we need to up the punishment a bit." The next thing I knew, my pants were down around my ankles and I was stretched out across his lap. Master Gareth hadn't put his cock back in his pants, so his wet tip was pressed against my naked side as I wiggled into place.

The ruler was in one of his hands, while his other one helped hold me in place. "You're such a bad girl, Liz."

"Yes, Sir."

"Never doing what I want you to do."

"No, Sir. Never."

"Now I have to mark your beautiful ass."

The first slap of the wood against my skin was fairly gentle. Master Gareth liked to test me, get me ready when we were about to use something we hadn't before. We'd long ago established my safeword, and I'd never had to use it. Hell, I was convinced that he knew my limits better than I did.

The ruler connected again with my ass, this time leaving a biting sting in its wake. A little yelp escaped me. Dammit, I shouldn't still react that way. It's not like this is a totally new thing, but man it really did hurt.

"Only a few smacks and your ass is already turning a lovely shade of red." He ran his fingers over the spot where the ruler had connected, pressing into the spots where the wood had left its mark. "You're so sensitive."

"Oh, I know it. Sir."

Another smack, this time to the other cheek. Yeah, I totally deserved that.

"You're still thinking too much, Liz." He set the ruler down on the table in my line of sight. "Something has gotten into you."

"I wish you would get into me, Sir."

Since Master Gareth had gotten over his reservations about taking our relationship to the next step, he'd really taken a shine to fucking me. I'd been pleasantly sore for many days after a sex-filled weekend last month. It was the first time we'd had sex beyond being in our Master and submissive roles.

I'd forgotten how much I'd loved that.

The rest of my thoughts evaporated as Master Gareth unleashed a series of spanks that crisscrossed both my ass cheeks and the backs of my thighs. The bite of pain dissipated and morphed into intense pleasure. All I could focus on was my breathing, the pounding of my heart, and the feel of Master Gareth's cock hot and hard against my side.

"That's my girl." He nudged my thighs apart just wide enough to slip his hand between. "Let's see if you're ready."

The touch of his cool fingers against my hot pussy sent a jolt through me. My moan was unstoppable.

"Nice and wet. Ready for me to fuck you." Master Gareth thrust two of his fingers into my pussy and let the knuckle of a third one press against my clit. "I wonder if I should let you come? You did interrupt my class. Should I be good to you?"

I clenched my muscles around his fingers. "Yes, Sir. *Please,* Master Gareth."

"Not yet."

Shit, I hated when he did this. "Please, Sir. I promise to be good. I won't bother your class ever again."

Smack! "Your promises mean nothing."

"I'll do better." *Smack!* "I won't bother you again." *Smack!* "I'll even do your marking for you."

"Suck my cock until I come, then we'll see."

My body shook as I carefully slid off his lap and took his cock in my mouth. I was past the point of being able to tease him. My legs shook as I bobbed my head up and down, sucking hard as I fisted his cock. Master Gareth was normally quiet when I was giving head. This time was no different. His hands found their way to my head, guiding my movements, encouraging me to suck harder and faster.

It wasn't until his thighs began to shake beneath me that I knew he was about to come. I closed my eyes and steadied my breathing in and out through my nose. The head of his cock swelled for a second before his hands tightened in my hair and his come filled my mouth. His body bowed forward as he curled over me. The shift in angle forced his cock even farther toward the back of my throat.

Black spots appeared in my line of sight as my need for air increased. I dug my nails into his thighs, warning him that there was a problem. Thankfully, he was with it enough to pull back, freeing me to suck in a gasp of air.

"Such a good girl." Before I could react, he picked me up and placed me on the desk where he'd sat a moment before.

I collapsed back against his desk, my legs splaying apart as Master Gareth thrust his fingers into me once again.

"I'm going to fuck you with my hand. Because unlike in the movies and books, I don't keep condoms in my office. Tonight, though . . . I'm going to fuck you raw."

He pushed two fingers as far as they'd go into me. The pace he set was fast and steady. My nipples were on fire, my ass hurt as my body moved in time against him. I'd been here before, this place where all I could do was give in and trust that Master Gareth would look after me.

It was awesome.

"I'm going to take one of the elastics off. Don't come."

Okay, not so awesome. I was really fucking close.

As he reached up with his free hand and fumbled with the band, I closed my eyes and tried to time my breathing with the movement of his fingers in me. The second the elastic came free, though, blood rushed from the point and the burning pain nearly pushed me over the edge.

I cried out and tensed. "Can't stop it!"

Master Gareth pulled his hand free of my pussy. "Don't you dare. Hold on."

Tears leaked from my eyes and rolled across my temple into my hair. "Can't stop."

"Yes, you can. One more elastic and then you can come. Liz? Do you understand?"

I recognized the words, but they weren't quite registering in my brain. More tears slipped down my face, which helped bring me back from the edge. "Yes."

"I'm going to take the band off and put my fingers back into your cunt. Only when I say so can you come. Liz?"

"Please hurry, Sir."

I loved that Master Gareth knew when I was doing my best to follow his directions, when the limits he'd set out for me were too much. He didn't push me farther and within a moment the second elastic pulled free and his fingers were back in my pussy.

I managed to hold off for two seconds before my orgasm slammed into me. The waves of pleasure started off strong, growing in intensity as he continued to milk my body. I didn't know if I was screaming or not, if I was even capable of that. My body became a lightning rod for my release, directed my orgasm throughout every atom of me.

Somehow, I didn't pass out.

Not sure why not.

Master Gareth—no, just Gareth now—helped me up and cradled me in his arms until I came down from my high. He placed the occasional kiss to my damp temple and stroked his thumb across my shoulder.

Finally, I was able to swallow and look up at him. "Hi."

His smile was barely a quirk of his lips, but his eyes looked to be dancing. "Hi."

"So, that happened." I shifted on the desk. "Ouch."

"We should get you dressed and back home. I want to put some cream on you and make sure I didn't do any damage. The ruler probably wasn't the best choice."

And that was what confused me. The girls at the office said that this was abuse. That the psychological marks he'd leave behind would be worse than the red marks on my skin that I'd finish the night with. But if it really was cruelty, he wouldn't care for me afterward, making sure I had ointment on a welt if necessary and water and a blanket.

Would he?

"Thanks."

"Hey, you okay?"

I wasn't about to ruin the moment by getting into my concerns with him. There'd be time for that later. "I'm good. Just been a long day."

Gareth frowned and I knew he wasn't buying it. Still, he didn't push me further. "How about we get takeout on the way back to your place?"

I perked up. Food was totally the way to my heart. "Oh, can we go to that new burrito place? That shit's so good."

"Sure." He tucked some of my hair behind my ear. "And maybe we can talk later. Once you're more yourself."

My stomach growled. "Sounds good."

As we got dressed and righted his office, I knew that I would put off having that particular conversation as long as I could. For the life of me, I didn't know what that said about me.

CHAPTER 14

"If I ask you a question, will you promise not to freak out?"

Connie stopped pulling her laundry out of our dryer and looked at me. "You know whenever you say something like that I freak out regardless?"

"I know. But I was hoping this time might be different."

I'd put off answering Gareth's questions about my mood the other night by filling him full of burritos, nacho chips, and homemade salsa. Then I insisted we watch the movie I'd gotten him for his birthday last month, even though we'd seen it twice already. The last thing I'd wanted to do was make Gareth feel that there was something wrong with our relationship, especially after how far we'd come after his own doubts about starting something new after the death of his wife. It was far better to suffer Connie's wrath than risk hurting him.

"You've got that look to you." She threw a towel at me for good measure. "Spill it, Liz."

God, I didn't want to insult my best friend. Her relationship with Stephen had been through its ups and downs over the years, enough for her to be sensitive to these types of questions. They were in a good place now with a wedding on the horizon. But I'd already opened this particular can of ick, so better to simply get on with it.

"The other day at work there were some women talking about the Simon Caldwell case."

Connie snorted. "That asshole should be thrown in jail and have the key blasted into space."

"I agree. But then they got to talking about the women and how they were being abused."

"Yeah, they were." Connie shut the dryer door closed with her hip. "He was totally taking advantage of them."

"But he claims it was rough sex."

"Sweetie, there's a difference."

"I know that." I did. It was something I thought about all the time. "But it got me worried about . . . you know."

"About how much you like it when Gareth spanks your ass."

"I hate it when you say shit like that." I threw the towel back at her. "They got talking about how people who like kinky sex like this are wrong in the head. Or that we've been abused and didn't know any better."

Connie didn't respond to that.

"Then, of course, I got to reading stuff online. Some articles claimed that we'd been rewired to think of pain as pleasure. That in itself wasn't normal. It's like we've been manipulated."

"People are assholes."

"I know that. And I know better than to listen to everything on the Internet. I guess . . ." I sat down cross-legged on the floor. "I'd never even questioned this. The whole Dom auction thing was such a weird and wonderful way to get into kink that it never occurred to me that maybe I shouldn't. That I was walking into something that wasn't good for me."

"Baby, I wouldn't let anything happen to you. Considering I was the one who introduced you to this, I would hope that you'd trust me."

"I do. Shit, I think I trust you more than myself. It's just . . ." I was being stupid.

"This is more than the Caldwell case." She sat down opposite me, mirroring my pose. "What's really wrong?"

"Nothing." Connie snorted, so I knew I'd have to give her more than that. "You know that promotion I'm going for?"

"Yeah."

"Work is going to be checking social media and stuff. They want to make sure they don't get any more sex freaks promoted."

"Jesus."

"So, on top of worrying that there is something wrong with me, I need to hide my extracurriculars from my bosses." My stomach turned as I spoke, and for the first time in a long time I couldn't look Connie in the eyes anymore.

"That's not fair. What you and Gareth do in the privacy of your home is none of their business." She let out a sigh. "I take it you were having some doubts about everything? Otherwise I can't see this bothering you."

As usual, Connie wouldn't let me take the easy way out. "I guess. I don't doubt Gareth, not even for a second. But I guess I'm worried that this is really the only thing we have in common. Most people don't start their relationships this way, with just sex." When it came down to it, I was worried that if the sex started to fade, if for some reason I wanted to walk away from the kink, that Gareth wouldn't have any reason to stay. But thinking that and saying it out loud were two completely different things. "I just don't want to be weird."

"Look, I don't know what to say. I don't think of myself as weird or abnormal. Though I might have had some issues as a kid that I didn't tell you about."

My head snapped up. "What?"

"It's . . . not something I discuss. Stephen knows, and that's really all that matters to me."

The fact that my best friend in the world was keeping something from me made my stomach turn again. "You know I'm always there for you."

"I know." She smiled and gave her head a little shake. "I'm fine and it's the past. I like to leave it there."

"Okay."

"Anyway, we're not abnormal for enjoying this type of sex. You were at Tail Whip and saw all the people there. If we're freaks, then we're a community of them. As long as everything is consensual, then you have nothing to worry about."

"I guess."

"You guess right. So, stop being so stupid, keep pictures offline, and take these towels to the closet, will you?"

The thought that I might be making a big deal out of nothing didn't do much to improve my mood. As I shoved each of the towels into their respective spots, I couldn't shake the feeling that as much as Connie might be right, maybe I wasn't cut out for this lifestyle.

Gareth and I had never discussed the possibility of having a relationship that didn't involve kink. Shit, I didn't know if that was something that he'd even be up for.

Logic would dictate that perhaps I should get my head out of my ass and talk to him about this and how I'd been feeling. No one had ever accused me of being logical. Better to let things be for now. If this was simply nothing more than an overreaction to a bunch of news reports, then I didn't want to screw things up with Gareth. We'd come too far for me to blow it now.

So, I was going to keep my mouth shut and continue to enjoy things.

Yup, that was totally what I was going to do.

Somehow.

*   *   *

I loved being naked. No, I wasn't model material—thicker thighs, a little extra meat on my ass, that little bulge around my belly—but I'd finally come to accept that I didn't need to try to fit a certain look. I was healthy, mostly happy, and currently naked as I vacuumed Gareth's living room carpet.

My mother would have given me hell if she saw me. Not for being naked in a man's house, but for doing his housework. Master Gareth had told me that this was part of my punishment for being thirty minutes late tonight. He didn't care that it was actually Stephen's fault for showing up late, which had thrown my entire timetable off. Personally, I figured it was just because Gareth didn't like to vacuum. One of these days I was going to call him on that.

I still didn't get why he'd have me do these "punishments" and then walk away. Wasn't the whole point of this to tease him while I dance around the coffee table and bend over to pick pillows off the floor? He'd always leave when I was preoccupied. Totally annoying.

The loud whirring of the motor died with a flick of the switch. I really hated vacuuming, but I was damn good at it. With a cursory glance around to make sure I hadn't missed anything, I wound the cord around the pegs and put it back in the closet. The television was still on, but the sound muted. Master Gareth had been watching something or other when I'd showed up, though he'd quickly abandoned the program upon my arrival. As I grabbed the remote to turn it off, I realized that he'd been watching the news.

Simon Caldwell was being led out of the courthouse with his lawyer, the two surrounded by a number of media looking for a statement. It was strange seeing him on the screen instead of walking through the halls on his way to some meeting or other. The normal, easy smile that he'd greet any passerby with was gone. His gaze locked on the ground below where he stood.

The ticker beneath him was a quote from one of the women who had claimed abuse at his hands: "He forced me onto the bed and spanked me until I had welts. It hurt for days."

God.

There had been more than one night where welts on my ass had turned out to be the precursor to a great evening. I flicked the sound on, for God only knew what reason. The newscaster spoke with enough gravitas to emphasis his point.

"The accused has denied any wrongdoing, claiming that he was upfront with the woman regarding his tendencies toward rough sex. In a statement to police, Mia Jones claimed that while she was a willing participant in the sex, Mr. Caldwell went beyond the realm of acceptable limits. She alleges Mr. Caldwell choked her until she passed out, where he continued the assault. Since those charges were laid against him, two other women have come forward with similar complaints."

I pressed the power button and stood staring at the blank screen. If this woman had walked into the situation with her eyes open and still ended up in trouble, then what the hell was I doing with Gareth? Maybe this was turning into one of the biggest mistakes of my life.

No, it couldn't be. Gareth was many things, but I couldn't believe that he'd hurt me. What Caldwell did wasn't what Gareth and I did. There was no reason for me to think otherwise.

Just because our version of sex and pleasure wasn't normal by a lot of people's standards, didn't mean I had to worry.

No, no reason at all.

I took a deep breath and steadied my nerves. "I'm all done, Sir."

Master Gareth didn't respond, which piqued my curiosity. If he wasn't talking that meant he was plotting my demise . . . well, something that I knew I'd enjoy. In either case, I knew that I'd need to find him. I gave my nose a scratch before I sauntered into his bedroom.

I still got a bit of a shock every time I came in here. I don't know what I'd been expecting the first time I'd been invited in, but the sage green walls, dark hardwood floor, and gigantic four-poster king-sized bed wasn't it. I was still convinced that he had hidden wall fasteners somewhere, though he'd yet to use them if he did. The room was sexy, though, totally my style.

And currently empty.

"Master Gareth?" Where the hell did he get off to? His place wasn't *that* big. "Sir?"

"Stop."

His voice wasn't raised, but the sternness in it had me freeze on the spot. "Yes, Sir."

I felt him come up behind me, the scent of his aftershave still clinging to him even after a full day's work. The wave of body heat that I'd normally feel against my skin from him was missing. He was probably still dressed, which got me excited. That was usually an indicator that we were about to get into something that would take us several hours. I'd had some of my best orgasms on nights like this. But unlike those previous times, I couldn't stop from being a bit unsettled.

His hands found their way to my shoulders, his fingers gripping me firmly, but not enough to hurt. The contact helped ease my tension. "Did you finish everything I asked of you?"

"Yes, sir. Vacuuming and straightening of the living room is finished." And now I hoped to get my reward. "Is there anything else you need, Sir?" *A blow job? Ball sucking? Pussy to your face?*

"Get on all fours on my bed. Don't move."

I couldn't help but smile. The only thing that saved me from a smack to my ass was the fact that I wasn't facing him. Without protest, I got into the position and waited. Master Gareth came around to the side of the bed so I was finally able to see what he had on.

The shock zipped through me, and there was no way I wasn't able to stare. Gone were his normal dress pants and shirt that he'd been wearing during our scenes. Instead, he'd somehow squeezed into a tight pair of leather pants and a black T-shirt that might as well have been a second skin. He'd stopped dressing up almost completely since we'd officially gotten together as a couple.

Wait a minute . . .

"That's the outfit you wore the night of the auction."

He cocked an eyebrow.

I rolled my eyes. "Sir."

"Yes, it is. I'm glad you remembered."

It was weird that I'd forgotten about how good he looked dressed this way. Dangerous, in control, and totally fuckable. How did I ever get the nerve up to bid for him at the auction? Master Gareth wasn't the type of man whom I'd normally think I'd have a chance with, would ever be an equal to.

Though were we really equals when it came to sex?

"Stop that."

I turned my head to look him in the eyes. "Stop what, Sir?"

"You're tense. If I didn't know better, I'd say you were nervous."

I sat up and rested my ass on my feet. My gaze slipped to the bed and I knew I was frowning. From day one Master Gareth had always told me that the submissives were the ones with the power in the relationships. That they could determine if a scene stopped or continued on, that the power of the safeword and the trust that they'd established with their verbal contract made it so.

For the first time in the four months that we'd been together, I truly wondered if that was the case. I'd never tested it. Not really.

Master Gareth frowned. "I'm pausing things. Are you okay, Liz?"

Such a simple question, with a very complicated answer. "I honestly don't know."

He sat down beside me on the bed. "You've been off for days now. Weeks even. I'd been hoping that you would talk to me on your own. I wanted to give you space. But now I'm asking. What's wrong? And please don't tell me nothing."

It shouldn't seem natural for me to be sitting naked beside him on his bed while he was fully clothed, but it was. I took his hand in mine, lacing our fingers. We didn't do this, hold hands. We didn't do a lot of things that typical couples did, and maybe that was the problem.

"I think I need a break." As soon as I said the words I felt sick.

Gareth tensed. "From us?"

"No, God no. Just from . . . kink. I think. I'm not sure."

He nodded and gave my hand a squeeze. "It's the Caldwell case, isn't it?"

"Yeah, I feel stupid because I never had any concerns about this when we first started. But every time I turn on the radio or the news it's there, in my face. People telling me that I'm a freak, or that my brain is screwed up, or that you're abusing me and I'm too dumb to notice. It's all anyone talks about at work. I can't say anything. If I agree with them, I'm lying. If I argue, then I risk my job."

I should say the rest, that I was scared that the basis of our relationship was faulty, but I just couldn't.

Gareth was normally a man who didn't react impulsively. I think it had to do with his academic leanings, his ability to look at a problem from different angles and find a way to deal with them. His quiet contemplation didn't unnerve me. If anything, at least I knew he was taking my concerns seriously and not simply brushing them off.

"If you have doubts about what we're doing, then I can't in good conscience continue." I couldn't help but hear the sad note in his voice. "If you don't trust me completely, then this is done."

Shit, it felt as though we were breaking up. "I don't want to lose you."

He smiled and patted my hand. "Me either."

"So, what do we do now?"

"You tell me." He looked me in the eyes. "As of this minute I'm not your Dom anymore. You need to tell me what you want."

The back of my throat tightened and it suddenly became difficult to breathe. "I want you. I want us to be a normal couple. Go on dates, have regular sex. Be together."

"Ah." He looked away. "Normal."

"You've done normal before. You told me you enjoyed it."

"I did."

We didn't say anything for several minutes. I was terrified that this was it between us, but I also knew that I couldn't continue on with the kink, not with how I was currently feeling. If Gareth was unwilling to try the normal thing, then there was a chance that this really was it for us.

He stood up but didn't let go of my hand. "I'm willing to do that."

Relief swept through me and I couldn't hold back my sigh. "Oh, good."

"But I think we should call it a night. I need time to think."

The last thing I wanted to do was leave him alone, but he'd done me the favor of trying this for me, it was the least I could do. "Sure. But can I see you tomorrow?"

"Maybe. Probably. I'll call you."

He didn't look at me as I got dressed, but neither did he leave me alone. I felt like shit for doing this to him, causing him this internal turmoil. When I pulled my socks on and was finally dressed, I put my hands on my hips. "Maybe I'm overreacting. I'm being stupid."

"No, you have concerns and they need to be addressed. In a way I'm surprised you haven't had some doubts before now." He pinched the bridge of his nose. "It's fine."

It really wasn't, but that's where I'd put us.

He walked me to the door and waited for me to get dressed. Before he opened the door, I leaned up and kissed him hard on the mouth. "Okay. Call me."

"Yeah, tomorrow."

I took transit home and managed to keep my shit together until I got into my place. I was greeted with the sounds of Connie's and Stephen's moans coming from her bedroom. That was the last straw for me. With tears streaming down my face I raced into my room, quietly shut the door, and fell onto my bed. I fell asleep at some point, my cheek pressed to my tear-soaked pillow.

CHAPTER 15

I was on pins and needles the next day. The last thing I wanted was to make matters worse by reaching out to Gareth before he was ready. He'd told me that he'd get in touch, so I'd have to trust that he'd do that.

Instead of pining by my phone, I took to cleaning the apartment. By the time Connie got up, I'd already scrubbed the kitchen and bathroom and had moved on to organizing the pile of DVDs and books that we'd shoved into the far corner of the living room.

"Holy shit, what's wrong?" Connie looked around, shocked. "You never clean. Like, ever."

"I just had the urge this morning. Go with it."

"Baby, I've known you forever. You *never* get the urge to clean. Just doesn't happen. Even Stephen doubts you're capable."

I sighed and dropped my chin to my chest. "I kind of freaked out on Gareth last night and told him that I wasn't sure I could do the kink thing anymore."

"You *what?*"

"Don't yell at me."

"I'm not yelling!"

"Yes, you are."

"Sorry." Connie made her way over to the couch and fell onto it with a groan. "What happened?"

I gave her a quick rundown of what happened, ignoring her when she'd swear. "I know, I screwed up."

"No, you didn't. Not really. If you weren't comfortable, then you were right to stop." She leaned forward. "Do you think he'll call?"

I'd spent the better part of the morning wondering the same thing. "I hope so."

"Stephen's asleep, but I can wake him up and have him call Gareth for you—"

"God, no. He asked for space and I'll give it to him. I owe him that much."

There was a knock on the front door that had us both looking. My heart began to pound when Connie got up to answer it. I couldn't tell you how, but I knew it was Gareth on the other side. When she opened up and invited him in, I had to force myself to my feet. Dread is such a melodramatic word, and yet, that was exactly how I felt when I laid eyes on him.

He wasn't smiling. He also wasn't dressed the way he normally would be on the weekend. His jeans were baggy and faded, worn through in various spots. It wasn't a store-bought distressed look either. These suckers were old. His light gray T-shirt wasn't much better. He didn't look like himself.

"Where the hell did you find those?" I struggled to my feet, ignoring the pins and needles in my legs. "Is that a ball cap?"

He looked down at it and frowned. "Yes. What's wrong with it?"

"I've never seen you wear one. In nearly half a year."

He shrugged. "I actually own more than one."

"Okay." Connie clapped her hands together. "This is awkward. So, I'm going to take some Pop-Tarts into the bedroom and hide there until you leave and it's safe to come back out." She spun around and did exactly that.

Oh, Connie.

Gareth cleared his throat. "I was thinking that maybe today we could spend some time together. Do some boring normal stuff for a bit. If you're up for it?"

I don't think his words registered at first. In my heart I'd been expecting him to break up with me, cut the ties that would hold him back from doing something that he loved. I had to shake my head to make sure that I wasn't imagining things.

"Really?"

"I'm not a beast, Liz. I'm a normal guy and can do normal things." The steel that once laced his voice was gone. In its place was a quality that I couldn't put my finger on. Regret? Detachment? No, not that. Something else.

"I never claimed you were." I crossed the room to stand in front of him. There were so many ways things could have gone between us. This was the one option that I'd hoped for but hadn't believed would happen. "Let me grab my coat and purse and we can head out."

This time he smiled, and for the first time since last night I saw a sparkle in his eyes. "Good. It was hard, but I managed not to plan the entire day. Just some ideas."

"I have a few, too."

"We'll do yours first."

Knowing him the way that I did, it was hard for him to give up all control. That wasn't what I wanted either. Still, we had to start somewhere on our journey to "normal."

"Okay. First stop is for coffee. I slept like ass and need a hit."

* * *

By the time noon rolled around, I was more than able to declare our experiment a failure. We'd walked around downtown Toronto, ducked in and out of stores as we ran some of the errands that I'd been putting off all week. We'd had lunch, though the decision-making process to figure out where we were going to go was excruciating. Gareth wouldn't tell me anything, make any decisions. I don't think he was doing it to be frustrating, he just simply didn't know how to act when he wasn't supposed to be in charge.

By the time dinner rolled around, the prospect of going to another restaurant had lost its appeal. I texted Connie to see if she was going to be at the apartment.

"What now?" Gareth was holding my bags with my purchases in them.

"Well, Connie and Stephen are going to the club tonight. That means the apartment is empty. I was thinking I could make you dinner. As a thank you for today. We could watch something on Netflix if you want."

"Sounds good."

I don't know if I thought he'd say no, but once he'd agreed the knots in the back of my neck loosened slightly. "Awesome. I have some stuff in the fridge that I can make into a decent meal. Unless you want to get takeout instead?"

Gareth chuckled. "Let's not go through that again. Whatever you want to make is good."

For the first time all day, the tension between us lessened. That feeling continued until we reached my place, where we dumped my purchases on the couch and I proceeded to make us some pasta. Gareth took control of finding us a movie to watch as we ate and by the time I brought our plates out, a bottle of wine tucked beneath my arm, our evening was ready.

"That smells great." He smiled as he shoveled in the food. "I found us a movie. Action thing."

He wasn't a big fan of action movies, preferring more art-house fare, but I loved them. "Cool. We can watch something different afterward."

The meal was consumed in silence and before the movie was even thirty minutes in, we were leaning together on the couch, his arm around my shoulder. It was comfortable. Easy. Something that we really hadn't done much of since we'd gotten together.

I wasn't completely convinced that I liked it.

Still, since this whole day was the result of my freak-out, the least I could do was see it through to the end. I snuggled in close and placed my hand on his chest just above his heart. The movie droned on, but I'd lost interest. I was more concerned with getting into Gareth's pants. Our aborted attempt at sex last night had left me more than a little hot and bothered, something that I hoped we'd be able to address now. Without taking my eyes off the television, I slid my hand down the front of his body to the waist of his jeans. He hadn't bothered with a belt, which made the task of sliding my hand beneath much easier.

"Liz?" His voice echoed in my head. "What are you doing?"

"Just go with it."

While there were a lot of things that I hoped might be different between us, our mutual love of blow jobs—me giving, him receiving—wasn't one of them. While a car exploded in the background, I gripped his hardening cock in one hand while I worked the front of his jeans open with the other. He lifted his hips while I pulled his jeans down, positioning myself on the floor between his thighs.

I licked up his cock, humming as I went. "You smell good."

"Showered."

"So considerate." I sucked the head of his cock into my mouth. "Have I told you that I really enjoy the taste of you?"

"Once or twice." His hands found their way to my head. "You're good at this."

"I know." I took him all the way down my throat, all the way to the back.

My mouth watered as I worked it up and down his shaft. His balls were already tight and I knew he was as turned on as I was. When I didn't think he could take anymore, I pulled back and got to my feet. "I think we should move this to the bedroom."

The television was off and Gareth was behind me, encouraging me along before I could blink. Once we shut the door, I turned on my lamp, giving us just enough light to see. "That will do."

"Strip." The command came from him in such a natural way that I nearly complied.

Instead, I turned to look at him. "No, not tonight."

He frowned. "What do you mean?"

"No telling me what to do. This is—"

"Right. Normal sex. Habit."

He genuinely looked sorry. It was cute. "It's all good. Why don't we both get naked and then have some fun?"

We watched one another as we removed our clothing. Normally Gareth was always at least partially dressed when we'd get together. It was a pleasant and highly arousing change to see him totally naked. His cock was fully hard now, a beautiful sight in the dim light. My pussy was wet and I was more than ready for him to take me.

The only problem was, I didn't know how best to move forward. Sex wasn't something that I'd had to think about beyond doing what Gareth asked of me for . . . four months now. Not that I'd forgotten what I'd done with other men before him, it just didn't seem as exciting.

I lay on the bed, shifting around so my head was on the pillows. With my legs spread wide, I beckoned in closer. "I think a little reciprocation might be in order."

Gareth was a talented man when it came to all things sex. Going down on me was no different from anything else. With his face stern and his gaze locked on my pussy, he moved into position so his mouth hovered above my clit. The rush of his breath had me shivering, knowing that some relief from the tension of the past two days would finally come to an end.

The first touch of his tongue against my swollen clit pulled a moan from me. He parted my nether lips with his thumbs as he suckled the nub. He wasn't gentle, but nowhere near as rough as he'd been in previous times. The steady lapping and suckling of my clit was pleasant, but I wasn't feeling that building intensity that would normally wash over me.

"Harder," I whispered as I tugged at his hair. "More."

He did as I asked, sucking harder, teasing me with his tongue and lips. On and on he went and slowly my body began to climb toward the release that had escaped me to this point. My body tensed and I squeezed my eyes hard, trying to concentrate on the feeling of pleasure, needing it to build.

Gareth lifted his head and replaced his mouth with his fingers in my pussy. "Relax. You're trying too hard."

"I'm not."

"You are. Just go with it. If you trust me I'll be sure to get you there."

He began to pump his fingers in and out of me. It was the same rhythm that he'd used back in his office. I let my mind drift back to that memory, pulling up as many of the details as I could manage. The sting of his hand as it connected with my ass. How exciting it was to be having sex in his office, a place where anyone could have interrupted. How much it hurt when he'd used the wooden ruler on me. The pain mixed with pleasure as my sensitive skin pressed against the wood of his desk when he licked my pussy.

Yeah, that was it. What I needed.

"That's it, baby. Just let go." He curled his fingers up and pressed against my G-spot.

He matched the flicks of his tongue with the movement of his hand. He turned his hand slightly so his thumb teased my clit just below where his mouth connected. I groaned and bucked my hips in an attempt to match his rhythm.

I was almost there. So fucking close that I could taste my orgasm. My body tensed as my muscles shook from the strain. I tried to grab hold of the sensation, to follow it to that magical place where I desperately wanted to go. The minute I did, the pleasure plateaued before reaching the peak. And in an instant it faded away.

"Fuck." I banged my head back against the pillow.

Gareth pressed his cheek against the inside of my thigh, kissing the skin gently. "You're too tense. If you don't relax, you'll never come."

"I know." Propping my body up with my forearms, I looked down at him. Shit, he looked disappointed. "I think I just need to feel you inside me."

"You're lucky I carry condoms on me now." His little smile had me relaxing. "Let me grab one."

I took advantage of his brief absence to refocus. I was clearly overly excited, something that hadn't happened to me in a long time. I mean, it used to happen quite frequently with some of my other boyfriends when we were having sex, but this was the first time with Gareth.

A few deep breaths and I was able to slow my heartbeat.

Okay, so I was definitely freaking out a bit here. He was right that I would never come if I just didn't let my mind go and enjoy this. He'd climb on top of me, and I knew the feel of his naked body against mine would be awesome.

By the time he'd gotten the condom, I knew I was ready to make things happen. "Hello, sexy."

He cocked an eyebrow. "Hi back at you."

"Sorry about that. I don't know why I was trying so hard."

"It's just different. From what we've normally done." He shrugged and ripped the condom packet open with his teeth.

It was fun to watch him roll the latex down his shaft, the little tip of the condom sagging to the side. "It looks like a droopy hat."

"A sexy droopy hat, I hope."

"Totally. Let's put it to good use."

I let my thighs fall apart once more, giving Gareth room to position himself between them. This time he climbed up and braced his hands on either side of my chest, balancing on one just long enough for him to guide his cock into my pussy.

I sighed as he thrust forward, filling me. "So much better."

Gareth didn't say anything. Instead he pressed his face to the side of my neck and began to slowly pump in and out of me. My clit was already sensitive from where he'd been sucking on it, and with each shift of his body against mine, the pleasure increased.

Wrapping my arms and legs around him, I placed a series of kisses, licks, and nips along the side of his neck and across his shoulder. The taste of his sweat filled my mouth, the scent of his aftershave filled my nose. His body was hot and hard as he worked me, pushing me closer to release.

I was able to feel the build-up of pleasure once more. Rather than chase it, I simply tried to experience it. Took note of how hard my nipples had grown as they rubbed against his chest hair. The jolt that went through me each time his body connected with my clit. Finally, I knew I was on the verge of release. I closed my eyes and let the orgasm crest until it spilled over. My moans echoed against Gareth's body and rang loud in my ears.

His thrusts increased in speed and intensity. His fingers dug into my shoulders, using my body as leverage. I held still, nearly holding my breath while I waited for him to come. Finally, he pressed his face against my throat, and let out a long, low growl as his body shuddered above mine. The full weight of his body descended against mine for a moment, and I took that opportunity to stroke his hair.

Gareth wasn't normally a talkative man during sex. Well, not unless he was giving me a bunch of directions to follow, but there was something different about the silence that fell between us now. He placed a kiss to my cheek, rolled off me with his hand holding the end of the condom.

"Be right back."

It was weird. We'd both come. We'd both had the opportunity to explore one another's bodies. Everything had been great.

So, why did it feel as though something had gone terribly wrong?

The rush of water from the bathroom was quickly followed by Gareth returning to the bedroom with a facecloth in hand. He gently nudged my thighs apart once more as he cleaned me up. It was by far the most intimate thing we'd done that night.

"Hey." I took his hand, ignoring where the warm, damp cloth fell. "That was nice."

"It was." He smiled, but the spark wasn't in his eyes.

I took a breath. There was a sour taste in the back of my throat that I tried to swallow down, but that refused to go away. "Are you okay?"

He laced our fingers together and cupped the top of my hand with his free one. "This was good for you? Was it normal enough?"

Dammit. "It was good, yes. You say normal like it's a terrible thing."

"Liz . . ." He closed his eyes and sighed. "You know I care for you. I love you. And those are words I never thought I'd say to another woman."

Tears began to build in my eyes. "I love you too."

"When Rachael and I first started engaging in BDSM, I never thought that it would become such an important part of who I am. It gave me permission to explore a part of myself that I held under wraps for most of my life."

Please don't say it. Please just, can we do this together?

"I've gone through a lot over the years. Had to reevaluate who I was as a person after Rache died. For good or bad, I'm a Dom. This is the lifestyle that I think suits me."

I closed my eyes. "I know."

"I don't think I can give you what you want. I don't think I can deny that part of who I am. Not if I want to be happy."

"I know." The tears were soaked up by my pillow. "I'm sorry."

"No, I'm sorry." He ran this thumb across the corner of my eye, brushing away the tears. "You know I would never be like Caldwell. Do something to hurt you. Really hurt you."

"I know you wouldn't."

"So, what's so wrong about continuing on? We've been good for four months. You even chased after me. Wanted *me*."

He was right. There hadn't been anything about what we'd been doing that had bothered me. But I couldn't get my head around the idea that despite everything we'd shared, there'd be a limit to what I'd be able to handle. The line between what we did in the bedroom and what our lives were outside of that would blur. I couldn't do my job and live my life as a total submissive. As much as I clearly liked kink in the bedroom, as much as I wanted Gareth forever and ever, I didn't know if this was simply a phase or who I really was.

Opening my eyes, I looked right at Gareth. "You're a good man. And I still want you."

"But?"

"But I'm not sure if I can do this long term. I mean, what does it say about me that I enjoy giving up all my control to someone else? Anyone else? It's like I've lost a piece of my identity. I don't want to change who I am."

Gareth nodded. "There's not much I can say to help fix that. Except to tell you that you haven't. You're still Liz. You still laugh and love those awful movies. You are a great friend, a loving partner, and a kick-ass pasta maker. I don't want to lose you."

I didn't want to lose him either. But I would be lying to both of us if I simply kept going forward with our relationship the way it was.

Silence stretched on between us for a moment before I sat up and wiped my face. "So, now what?"

"I don't know. What do you want?"

There was the million-dollar question if I ever did hear it. And the answer was something that neither of us would want to hear. "I think I need to take some time for myself. Figure things out."

Gareth nodded. "For the best. I'll give you some space." He reached out and took my hand in his. "I'll miss you."

God, this was such a shitty idea. "I'll miss you too."

"Lay back." He gathered the strewn bedding and rearranged it so I was now comfortably tucked in. "Good night, Liz." And he placed a kiss to my forehead.

I never heard the door to the apartment close. I was too busy crying.

CHAPTER 16

"Jesus Christ, Liz. Will you get your ass out of the apartment?"

Connie had stepped in front of the television, blocking my view of the cooking show I'd been watching. "Dude, you're blocking Bobby Flay."

"Fuck Bobby Flay." She crossed her arms and glared at me. "You haven't left here other than to go to work in three weeks. You're being a complete idiot and ruining my sex life. Stephen doesn't want to do anything when he knows you're here and upset."

I'd heard it from her before. *Gareth cares for you. He'd never abuse you that way. You're being an idiot. . . .*

"God, Liz." Connie threw her hands in the air and marched back to the kitchen.

I knew she was right. I knew in my heart that not seeing Gareth was only hurting me. But as much as my heart told me this, the logical part of my brain knew that if I couldn't figure this out on my own, come to terms with the fact that yes, I'm a bit weird and like to be beaten during sex, then I would only bring doubt to our relationship. That would lead to hurt feelings and arguments. And *that* would lead to us hating each other.

Yeah, that thought certainly didn't get my ass off the couch.

Bobby Flay eventually morphed into some show about food trucks, which got my stomach rumbling. Eating was probably a good idea. I pushed myself off the couch with great effort and sauntered to the kitchen.

Connie was nowhere to be seen, which was a small blessing. I knew she meant well, but I couldn't take her pressuring me either. I'd finished making my sandwich and had taken my first bite when Stephen came into the apartment.

"Hey, Liz. Where's Connie?"

I nodded my head toward her bedroom and took another bite.

Rather than disappearing immediately, Stephen joined me in the kitchen. I knew I was in trouble when he leaned against the counter beside me, his arms crossed and his gaze narrowed. "Are you still moping?"

I swallowed hard. "I don't mope."

"Please. If you were my sub I would have flogged you for lying that poorly." He lightly shoved at my shoulder. "But I'm not. Your real Dom has been moping as well."

"Gareth doesn't mope."

"Well, he's been doing a pretty good impression of it down at the club for the past few weeks. Which reminds me." He reached into his pocket and pulled out his phone, pressed a few buttons, and handed it to me. "Here you go?"

"What the hell are you—"

"Liz?"

My mouth fell open and I glared at Stephen. "Gareth?"

"I've done my best to give you space. I've reminded myself daily that things will never work between us if you don't come to this on your own. I refuse to pressure you, but I need an opportunity to make a case for my side of things. If you are okay with it, I would like you to come down to Tail Whip so we can talk. It's someplace public, neutral. You know it and know all the security that's in place to keep you safe."

Gareth wasn't normally much of a talker, so I knew there would be more to it than that. "Maybe."

"I'll be there all night. From seven until close. If you don't show up, then I know that we're done, and while that will hurt, I'll accept it. If you do come, I want you to wear the outfit that you did the night of the Dom auction."

Stephen held the phone steady against my ear, which I was suddenly grateful for. I was able to shove my shaking hand into my pockets. "Okay. If I come."

"Thank you, Liz."

I nodded at Stephen, who pocketed his phone. "You going to go?"

"I don't know. Maybe." I hated feeling so torn about something that had brought me so much joy. "I really miss him, and I don't want him to change because of me, but I don't know if I can do this."

"Why? You'd really started to embrace that side of yourself. No, it's not for everyone. But it looked to be the thing for you."

"I'm not sure what that says about me."

"It doesn't need to say anything. You're consenting. He's consenting. You can stop if and when you want to and he respects that." Stephen wrapped his arm around me and gave me a quick hug. "I know that thing with Caldwell has you freaked. And it should. He took advantage of those women. He should be punished for what he did. But that has nothing to do with you and Gareth."

"Doesn't it?

"No, you and Gareth are in a relationship. You talk to one another, have more in common than just BDSM. It's only a part of who you are, not the defining quality of either you or your relationship."

"I know—"

"And," Stephen raised his voice ever so slightly, "it's important to remember that there are jerks out there who have no problem abusing women. They don't use BDSM as an excuse for that."

"You're right."

"I think you owe it to yourself to go. If for no other reason than so you're certain that you're walking away from him for the right reasons."

With one final hug, Stephen grabbed an apple from the counter and wandered off to Connie's bedroom.

Leaving me alone to make a decision.

* * *

It was funny, but Gareth and I hadn't come to Tail Whip all that often in recent months. While it had been the place where our relationship had started, it was still a place where I felt more of an outsider than a member. Plus, Gareth had all the toys a girl could possibly want. I wasn't big into exhibitionism, so going to the club was a take-it-or-leave-it thing.

The Tail Whip was in full swing by the time I'd arrived.

Dance music thumped through the speakers, a primal rhythm beneath the sounds of sex. Laughter mixed with moans and the occasional crack of leather surrounded me as I made my way to the bar.

My corset was stiff and pressed against the top of my jeans as I walked. The motion caused my breasts to shift beneath the stiff fabric, making my nipples hard. The air of the club was cool against my skin, dragging a shiver through me. It was odd being here alone. It felt as though I were on display, an offering for any Dom who might be interested.

Not that I was. If I was going to go back down this road, there was only one man whom I'd even consider going on the journey with.

I leaned against the bar and waited for the young woman to slide over to me. She was also wearing a corset, a black leather one that put her breasts on full display. She'd been around the club for as long as I'd been coming here. What the hell was her name? Stacey? Sara?

"Sonya, can I get a glass of water?" I beamed when her name popped into my head. I really needed to make more of an effort to remember that sort of thing.

"Sure thing." She smiled as she filled the glass with ice before topping it up with water.

The glass was cold and sweaty as I wrapped my hand around it. "Thanks. Hey, you haven't seen Master Gareth by chance?"

She winked at me. "He's a hard man not to notice. You're his sub, right?"

"Something like that." I honestly had no fucking clue what we were anymore.

"Well, he was here earlier. I haven't seen him in a bit, though, so God only knows where he is. Maybe check with one of the dungeon monitors. They're better at keeping tabs on people."

Right. I should have thought of that. "Thanks, Sonya."

The dungeon monitors were men and women who kept an eye on the people at the club. They made sure that everyone was following the rules, that everyone was safe, and if anyone did have a problem, there was someone there to help. I had no idea if other clubs were like that, but it certainly made me feel safer.

The few times we'd been here, I hadn't really had any reason to speak to any of them. Gareth had always respected my limits, well, the ones that he knew I didn't want to be pushed past. Now approaching the guy closest to me, I couldn't help but feel a little nervous. "Excuse me."

The man had arms so big that I swore his biceps were larger than my head. *'Cause that's not scary at all.* "Hello, little lady. Is there a problem I can help with?"

"Nothing bad. I'm just looking for Master Gareth. He asked me to come find him."

He nodded and flicked a switch on a cord hanging from his shoulder. "Duncan here. I have a little sub looking for Master Gareth. Any sightings?" Someone must have spoken because Duncan nodded. "Thanks."

I couldn't tell you why I was so nervous. I hadn't been forced to come here. This was purely my decision. And yet the moment Duncan smiled down at me, I developed a serious case of *holy shit, I should totally just run* syndrome.

"Do you know where the private rooms are?"

I should have known that's where he would want to meet. "I do."

"Are you sure you're okay?" The frown Duncan wore gave him an aura of menace. "Master Gareth is a good guy, but if you're being pressured—"

"Oh, God no. I've just been freaking out a bit recently. He's been . . . well, really awesome."

Duncan nodded. "A lot of people have been off with all that shit in the news. Caldwell using our lifestyle as an excuse. I remember that he tried to get a membership here once but management kicked his ass to the curb." Duncan leaned in, and despite the noise he lowered his voice. "Your Master Gareth is a good man. I know I'm not supposed to say stuff like this, but I don't think you need to worry."

"I know."

"Well, you better get moving, then. Unless you're in full brat mode tonight. In which case, take your time." He gave me a wink and returned to his post.

This was it. The point where I had to make a decision about me, Gareth, and where we were going to go from this point on.

I took a breath. Then I took another. Finally I straightened my shoulders and made my way to the private rooms. The dungeon monitor at the entrance to the hallway nodded as I approached.

"He's in the Blue Room."

"Thanks."

The hall wasn't long, but each step increased my nerves. It was a weird mix of excitement and fear, the pressure of not knowing exactly what Gareth had planned.

No, not Gareth. Not here.

This was Master Gareth and I better be ready to face him.

The door to the Blue Room was shut. I knew the handle wouldn't be locked, but I still hesitated to try it. I could still change my mind, walk away.

Not that I would.

Because memories of that first night came flooding back. Master Gareth giving me time to turn around and leave before things got started. His conversation with me, trying to learn who I was, wanting to make sure that I'd get as much pleasure as I could out of the experience. Little did either of us know how much our lives were going to change as a result of that auction.

"This is stupid." I let out a huff, reached for the handle, and pushed the door open.

Master Gareth was standing behind a chair that was positioned in the middle of the room. His black T-shirt fit just as well now as it had four months ago. The leather pants still hugged his thighs perfectly and made me promise myself to be better about going to the gym on a more regular basis.

I stepped fully into the room and closed the door quietly behind me. I didn't need to be told what to do, this wasn't my first rodeo after all. Still, it was odd not having him giving me directions. I carefully pulled off my heels and walked them over to the bench along the side of the room. Things had changed a bit in here since the last time we'd played, but the details weren't critical.

Only Master Gareth was.

"Leave the rest of your clothing on and come sit in the chair." The edge of his voice left little room for negotiation.

My jeans were a bit tight, so when I sat down on the chair I had to fight the urge to spread my legs. While it might have been more comfortable, sprawling would have given him the impression that I was relaxed. And I so wasn't that.

"I'm pleased you came. That you took your time deciding." He remained behind me, speaking over the top of my head. "I think it's time that we get back to basics. There've been some changes in your behavior recently that I'm not pleased with."

"Sorry, Master—"

"No, no Master or Sir or anything. We're not there yet. We are back at square one. The beginning. There are things we need to discuss and negotiate before I'll agree to be your Master again. Understood?"

"Yes." I nearly didn't cut off the *Sir* at the end of the sentence. It had become so natural, it felt as though a part of me were missing.

"The night of the auction you were brand-new at this, but you took to things easily. I want to revisit that. I want you to think about your reasons for being here that night. What brought you to the charity auction?"

"You know why." Yeah, that didn't come off bitchy at all. "Sorry."

"It's fine." Master Gareth circled around in front of me and dropped to a squat. "Remember, we're starting over. Just like that night." Just like he had then, he started rubbing small circles with his thumb on the inside of my knee. Before when my body had reacted, it was simply from the excitement of the unknown. Now, though, my clit pulsed and I couldn't stop from squirming in my seat. I knew what those hands could do. How talented his mouth was.

"So, why are you here, Liz?"

I licked my lips like I always did when I got nervous. "I'm here because I'm curious."

"No, you were curious back then. That's not the reason you're here tonight."

I sometimes really hated how perceptive he was. "You're right."

Normally, I would remain passive and let him lead me along. But that passivity had been most of the problem for the past few weeks. If I wasn't the one to take some action, then I knew I'd always question myself. Reaching down, I covered his hand with mine, keeping us connected.

"I'm caught between two worlds. I love what we've been doing in the bedroom. Since we've gotten together, my sex life has become something amazing. I've been able to do things that I didn't know were possible. I love that and I don't want to lose it."

He gave me that small smile of his but didn't interrupt me.

"But I'm greedy. I want the typical relationship stuff, too. We started off so weirdly. I mean, who buys a man for a night, charity auction or no? It's messed up. And then we were just doing scene things and then the movies and hanging out and stuff. It's like we accidently backed into a relationship."

"We did go about things in the wrong order."

"Right? It's crazy." I leaned in and pressed my forehead against his. "I don't want to lose you. I love you. But I need to somehow mesh these two worlds together."

We stayed like that for a bit, leaning against each other. Gareth eventually moved, rubbing the tip of his nose against mine.

"When I first started getting into BDSM, I was married. We'd already done the courting and this was the next step for us." He pulled back enough so I could really stare into his eyes. "I didn't want to admit to being scared to move past my wife. Each step we take is bigger than the last. What we shared made it easier for me to get involved. And make no mistake, Liz, I'm involved."

The shiver that ripped through me was equal parts desire and anticipation. "I want regular dates."

"Agreed."

"And floggings. I really want to keep the floggings."

"Of course."

"And office sex. I *really* liked the office sex."

"We'll have to see about that. You were all I could smell for days after." Master Gareth cupped my cheek. "I don't want to take away what we have. I want to build on it. You know me well enough to realize that sometimes I drag my feet. Not because I don't want to move forward, but because I'm scared to lose the past."

"I've said this before, but it bears repeating. I'm not Rachael. But I'll never force you to choose between us."

"Which is one of the reasons why I love you."

The grin bloomed across my face. "I love you too."

The smile dropped from his face, but the sparkle in his eyes remained. "Rules."

"Yes, Sir." I did love his rules.

He stood up, crossed his arms, and stared down at me. "Scenes will no longer be assumed. They must be negotiated ahead of time. Dates will happen." He cocked an eyebrow. "I will not be the only one planning those."

Yep, I really fucking loved him.

"I'm letting you know that things are about to get kinky. If you want to stop tonight, please say so right now."

I took my corset off instead.

"I'll take that to be an acceptance. From this point on the only way to stop the evening will be for you to say your safeword. Please tell me what it is."

"Book."

He smirked again. "Very well. You will refer to me as Master or Sir for the rest of the evening. Remove the remainder of your clothing and put it by your shoes. Then return to me."

"Yes, Sir."

The last time I got naked in this room I was a nervous wreck. My hands still shook, but this time with anticipation. Master Gareth was gathering items from the toy chest in the far corner of the room. I really wanted to peek at what he had in mind for me tonight, but that took some of the fun out of it. Rather than bounce on my toes beside him, I stood silent off to the side. I loved being a bit of a brat, but tonight I wanted nothing more than to be a good girl.

Master Gareth turned to face me, a set of leather cuffs in each hand. "Come here."

Holding out my arms as I stepped closer, I kept my gaze lowered. "Yes, Sir."

"Tonight is about remembering why you came here originally. What you enjoy about being restrained, spanked, fucked. Tonight is about you, Liz. Rediscovering who you are and accepting it."

I nodded. My throat had tightened from an unexpected rush of emotions. Dammit, I hated when he knew exactly what to say to make me cry.

The leather cuffs were a comfort around my wrists. They were tight enough to feel as though I were being hugged, but loose enough that I wouldn't lose circulation. Once they were in place, I remained still, knowing there would be more to come.

Master Gareth cupped my left breast, lowering his mouth to suck my nipple. I sucked in a breath through my nose and did my best to stand still. My nipples had always been super sensitive. Sometimes it was easier to take the pain he'd inflict on them than the gentle pleasure. The pleasure roared through me, too much to actually be enjoyable. It crested and vanished as he released me.

"So responsive." Then he bit down lightly on the peak.

There was no way I was stopping the moan that time. My pussy was wet and my clit swollen and all he'd done was cuff me and suck my nipple.

So going to be a fun night!

This time when he pulled away, he grabbed hold of my wrist and pulled me over to the restraints hanging from the ceiling. "Hands up."

As much as you prepare your body for this, every time it feels a bit different. I'd been tense for weeks, and my body ached. The muscles in my shoulders and upper back protested the sudden change in position as they were stretched up. My feet were perfectly flat, which gave me room to be able to adjust.

"Stand still." The edge was back to his voice. Now the real games were going to begin.

I lowered my gaze, closed my eyes, and got my breathing under control. Master Gareth gave me the time I needed to get into my proper headspace.

Well, almost enough time.

The unexpected slap to my ass drew a yelp from me.

"Eyes open. I want you to see everything I'm doing. I want you to know that it's me. That what I'm doing is exactly what you want." He held up a long, flat paddle. "We're going to start with this."

I licked my lips and nodded. "Whatever you want, Sir."

Master Gareth walked two slow circles around me. He touched me randomly, scraped his nails along various bits of my skin. My mind couldn't help but try to anticipate where the next caress or pinch would come. His fingers were then replaced with the soft scrape of the paddle along my back. The wood was well polished, sliding easily across my skin. It was cold as he ran it down the length of my back to the swell of my ass.

Instinctively, I held my breath, waiting for the sting of wood against flesh.

It didn't come.

Instead, Master Gareth continued to use it to draw lines down the backs of my legs, up the sides of my thighs, across the tops of my breasts. The longer he went on, the more he teased me, the more aroused I grew. My body shook and I had to fight harder to keep still, to not squirm away from the contact.

I lost track of how many times he circled me. I had to focus on a spot on the wall—an O-ring—so that I wouldn't get dizzy. My skin adjusted to the temperature of the room, making me hyperaware of his body heat each time he stepped close.

The paddle was pressed to my ass. The face was long enough to cover both cheeks, but not wide enough to touch my lower back or the tops of my thighs. Master Gareth held it there, and I knew he was doing what he needed to mentally be ready for what was to come.

The first slap of wood against skin was merely a testing blow. It wouldn't have hurt even the newest of submissives. Master Gareth always gave me a little tap to say, *Hey, this is happening now.* I relaxed my muscles and let gravity pull my chin toward my chest.

The second slap hurt. I cried out at the surprising bite of the pain. It woke me from my haze, pulled me back to the bright light that was Master Gareth. It felt as though a thousand small creatures had nipped at my ass all at once, leaving a sting in their wake.

The third slap was just as strong, the pain as bright.

The fourth, fifth, and six came in such rapid succession that I couldn't keep up with it. I tried to squirm away, move to avoid what was coming. Master Gareth grabbed my waist with one of his large hands and held me still.

The seventh slap brought a numbness that seeped into my muscles. The pain dulled and I was left with warmth that traveled through my body to my cunt.

Master Gareth walked around to face me. Using the edge of the paddle, he lifted my chin, forcing me to look him in the eyes. "You are so strong. Not many people could take what I'd just given you."

My heart pounded from his praise. "Thank you, Sir." My voice was ragged but clear.

He slid the long edge of the paddle down my body, between my breasts and across my belly button. "You know how to stop this. One word and I'll free you. You can walk away and I'll think nothing less of you."

"Yes, Sir. I won't do that."

"But you can." He moved the paddle edge between my legs, carefully pressing it to my clit. "You are in control. Always."

I gasped as he slowly increased the pressure on my clit. It would be so easy to give in, to let myself get swept up with the pleasure and come. Master Gareth wouldn't be pleased, but he would understand. But I wanted to do this right, for both our sakes. I held on, breathed through the growing pleasure, and distracted myself as best I could. Finally, Master Gareth removed the paddle and the pressure eased.

"Good girl."

Normally, this would be the time where he'd haul out the nipple clamps to torture me. He knew that I loved it, even when I was cursing him for inflicting them on me. But other than the paddle, he didn't seem to have anything else ready to use on me.

"Liz, I need you to hold still."

That was all the warning I got before he lined the paddle up with my left breast and gave it a smack.

"Aww!"

My nipple stung in a weird way. It hurt, but so did the rest of my breast. Before I could recover from the shock, he grabbed the now super-hard nipple between his finger and thumb and pinched hard.

I nearly came.

He then shifted position and repeated the actions on the other side. As he pinched me, I couldn't help but squeeze my thighs together. The added pressure on my clit was almost enough to push me over the edge.

"No!" He released my nipple and kicked my feet apart. "Don't you fucking dare."

"Please, Sir. Master Gareth . . ."

"You know better. I'm the one who lets you come. I'm the one who pushes you over. Me."

"Yes, Sir." *Fuckety, fucking, fucker.*

He disappeared for a moment, gone behind me to the toy chest. The spacer bar wasn't much of a surprise on his return. He quickly adjusted the bar and secured the cuffs to my ankles. Now there was no way in hell I'd be able to do anything.

"I hate you. Sir."

He slapped the inside of my thigh. "You don't."

Master Gareth continued his torture for so long, I lost track of how much time had passed. He'd switch from slapping my ass and the tops of my thighs with the paddle to lightly caressing and kissing the tender skin. Occasionally he'd bite my ass and I'd cry out. Pain and pleasure became mixed until I couldn't tell the difference.

"I'm going to try something different now."

The long, thin flogger tip teased the skin between my shoulder blades. Fuck, it had been a long time since he'd done that to me. My cunt throbbed, and I knew that the lightest of touches would be enough to make me come. If I was really lucky, he'd use the handle to rub me off and make me scream.

Yeah, right.

At first the taps of the flogger against my back were light. Nothing more than teasing kisses of leather strands against skin. I couldn't tell how wide the leather tendrils were, but they felt heavy, thick. That was the kind I enjoyed. He ran the flogger across my shoulders so the multitude of tips caressed the side of my neck and the tops of my breasts.

"I've wanted to do this to you for a week now."

I moaned. Master Gareth on a mission was always a good time.

"Those are the noises I want to hear. Be loud, Liz. Show me how much you're enjoying this."

Unlike with the paddle, Master Gareth was establishing a pattering with the blows. Right shoulder, left side. Left shoulder, right side. With each pass he increased the pressure, amped up the intensity of each blow. The touches morphed from light caresses, to gentle slaps, to biting stings.

"You should see your back, Liz. Your skin is turning red. It will match your ass soon."

I couldn't hold my head up any longer and let gravity pull my chin down toward my chest once more. The blows rained down on me, the pain causing me to relax more than anything else. I couldn't think about anything beyond the moment.

There was no pressure from work.

No fear of judgment.

No feelings of inadequacy.

No fear that Master Gareth would do anything to hurt me.

There was nothing but his sure touch and the arousal that burned me from inside out.

Master Gareth stopped and I was vaguely aware of him moving around before me once more. Using both his hands, he cupped my cheeks and looked me in the eyes.

"There's my girl." His voice was barely a whisper. "You're amazing."

He rubbed tears from my cheeks with his thumbs. I wanted to say something, thank him for bringing me to this place of peace, but I'd lost the ability to speak. Not that it mattered, because he knew. I could tell from the gentleness of the kisses he pressed to my forehead. The loving way he held me up as he released my arms from the chain that held them up.

If I'd been more with it, I would have been impressed by the way he scooped me into his arms while my legs were still splayed apart by the spacing bar. Instead, I pressed my face to his T-shirt and breathed in the smell of his sweat.

"I'm going to set you on the chair, Liz. I need to get the bar off. Don't you dare fall off."

I probably would have done exactly that if it hadn't been for the jolt of pain as my ass connected with the wood. Instead, my eyes popped open and I moaned. "Need to come."

He slapped the inside of my thigh.

"Sir. Need to come, *Sir.*"

"You will. When I say you can."

While I loved him, I really hated him at times.

"Stop your growling or I'll string you back up." Another slap to my thigh, but it was more of a love tap than anything else.

The spacing bar clanged as he tossed it away from the chair. He'd left the leather cuffs around my wrists and ankles in place, making my limbs feel heavier than normal. Rather than move me from the chair, Master Gareth pushed one of my legs to the side of the chair, while he threw the other one over his shoulder.

"Fuck. I've never seen you this wet before." He ran a finger through the stubble of my pubic hair and across the seam between my thigh and my body. "Your clit is huge. Red. Your pussy glistening."

I could see it in my mind's eye, my body spread open for him, waiting to be consumed.

Thankfully, he didn't make me wait long.

My eyes closed before I felt him move close to my pussy. Hot huffs of his breath blew across my cunt as he moved in. He liked it when I kept my arms still, restrained. But I couldn't. I wanted to feel the softness of his hair around my fingers. Clumsily, blindly, I reached for him. He didn't protest, instead lowering his mouth to my clit and licking a long swipe up.

I groaned and curled my fingers into his hair. I didn't care if I was hurting him. I couldn't think beyond *need, want, now.* Another slow pass of his tongue across my clit and I cried out. I shifted, sending another jolt of pain through my body. My ass and back were on fire. My pussy electric with desire. I needed to come before I combusted.

"Hold on, baby." Another gentle lick. "Hold on for me."

I would rather be subjected to the lashes from a hundred Doms than be forced to hold back an orgasm. My body shook and I felt beads of sweat form on my face, chest. It was too much for me to take, too hard not to get swept up by the waves.

"Just a bit longer." His words were blades against me, stinging.

He kept his mouth closed but shifted his body. I nearly wept when I felt the press of his fingers to my pussy. Gently, he teased my opening. Tiny thrusts that barely made their way inside me. I held my breath, knowing it was only a matter of time, moments before he'd finally give me what I wanted, what I needed. My head began to swim, but I waited.

Master Gareth must have sensed that I was on the edge, that there was no way I could stop from falling. From one heartbeat to the next I went from pain to pleasure. He simultaneously sucked hard on my clit as he thrust two fingers into me.

I came. I screamed. My body exploded as pleasure obliterated me and left me barely conscious. Pleasure tore me apart, making me aware of everything—my nipples, my throat, the raw skin of my back and ass. I dug my fingers into his hair and squeezed, forcing his mouth harder against my pussy. The last thing I wanted was for him to move, to break that connection and end the orgasm.

All the air left my lungs and I was unable to make any noise. I tried, but it felt as though every muscle in my body was squeezing and refused to give. Finally, the pleasure crested and my body gave. I sucked in a lungful of air, cried out, and collapse back.

"Jesus." Master Gareth cupped my inner thighs with both his hands. "Jesus."

"Fuck. Me." I would have begged more if I had the energy. No way *that* was going to happen.

Master Gareth was on his feet tearing at the opening of his leather pants. I couldn't move but managed a deep groan as his cock sprung free from its prison. He fished a condom foil from his pocket before shoving the leather down his legs.

"I'm going to fuck you hard. Right there in the chair."

Not needing to move was such a fantastic idea.

The moment he rolled the condom on, he grabbed my legs and positioned me so my ass barely connected with the chair seat. For a moment I thought the angle would be too awkward for him, but clearly he was determined to make this work. He slammed his cock into me with a single hard thrust, grabbed the back of the chair on either side of my head, and proceeded to fuck me.

Scared that I'd move and cause us both harm, I managed to find the strength to clutch his biceps and held myself as still as I could. With my legs spread wide, his pelvis came into full contact with my clit on each thrust. My body was still alight from my orgasm, my pussy oversensitive. I could feel the slide of his cock inside me, stretching the skin, encouraging my arousal to rise again.

I couldn't resist even this unspoken request.

As he'd thrust forward, I began to buck my hips up to meet him, increasing the pressure. Master Gareth looked down, his eyes hooded and his mouth parted. "Liz?"

"Again." I didn't need to say any more.

Master Gareth slowed his thrusts, meeting my rhythm. He started to roll his hips, grinding down a bit harder each time. My body responded, my pussy grew wetter, and the pleasure began to grow again.

"I can't hold back long." He swallowed hard. "Come for me. Do it, Liz."

The urge to close my eyes and focus on the sensations was strong, but that wasn't what I wanted this time. I needed to see him, his face, burn into my memory that this was *Gareth,* the man who loved me. The man who looked after me. The man who would stop, who *did* stop when I needed him to.

The man whom I loved more than anything.

I leaned in and placed a kiss to his cloth-covered chest, just above his heart. "I love you."

He groaned. "Love you too."

And then he came.

He threw his head back, crying out so loud that I wouldn't have been surprised if the dungeon monitor came in to check on us. His thrusts became erratic, nearly painful as he rode out his release. That was all it took to push me over the edge once again. Pressing my forehead to his chest, I let my second orgasm take me. Nowhere as powerful as my first one, I was able to enjoy the pleasure as it washed through me.

Finally, Master Gareth pulled free from me and slipped to his knees. "Fuck."

I don't know why, but I started to laugh. I hadn't been this happy in weeks.

"Dear God, she's losing it." But he started to chuckle as well.

"You fucked me crazy. This is totally your fault."

"I'm not to blame for this. You were nuts before we started." He groaned as he got back to his feet. "Clearly I need to do more squats at the gym. Let me get some cream for your back."

It wasn't until he walked away toward the toy chest when it hit me. "This is different."

"What is?"

"This . . . after."

He didn't say anything until he came back with a jar of something that I knew would feel amazing on my back.

"I've been thinking." He helped me up and took my spot on the chair before encouraging me to sit on his lap. "How you said you needed normal along with the kink."

"Yeah?" I didn't have a clue where he was going with this.

"The one thing that we'd always done after a scene was stay in our roles. I was Master Gareth, looking after his sub, tucking you in bed and leaving for home."

It was one of his more annoying habits. The few times I could convince him to stay the night, he always continued to treat me as his sub. Not that I was complaining. He always made good coffee in the morning. "I told you that you didn't need to do that."

"I know. I think it was my way of keeping some distance still." He rubbed the cream into my back in firm circles. "I'd created this divide in my mind between Master me and everyday me. Honestly, I hadn't thought much about it."

That made sense. "We really have gone about this whole relationship thing weirdly."

He pulled me back against his chest and swung my legs to the side. Cradled against him, I was able to relax completely. "I have a proposal. Something that I think will help us resolve the weirdness."

"I like your proposals." I teased his nipple through his shirt.

"Move in with me."

I looked up so fast that I nearly caught his chin with the top of my head. "*What?*"

There was a sparkle in his eyes that set my heart thumping. "You wanted normal. We've been together for a while now. It's the next *normal* step."

Moving in. Him and me. Master and submissive. "And you wouldn't expect me to be in submissive mode all the time?"

He ran a finger down my cheek. "I know this might be hard for you to believe, but I do like normal, too. I miss you when you're not with me. It would be nice to come home and know you'll be there as well."

"And we can have kinky sex whenever we want? Because I've come to the realization that I really love this shit."

"I'll master you every night. And make you coffee every morning. We'll be clear about boundaries. I want you to have peace of mind *and* kinky sex."

"You really know how to woo a girl." I pressed my head to his shoulder and sighed.

"So that's a yes?"

"You thought there was a chance that I'd say no?"

"I did. You are a wonderfully unpredictable woman. It's one of the things I love about you."

"I love you too. And yes, I'll move in with you." In that moment, everything slotted into place. My world righted and I knew that we would be okay. "Just one thing. You'll have to break it to Connie."

Gareth chuckled. "I don't think she'll be too broken up about it. Stephen has wanted me to get you out of there for months now."

"I should have known you two were scheming." Connie and Stephen would be happy. Gareth and I would be happy.

Everything was awesome.

I kissed the side of his throat. "Take me home."

Acknowledgments

This is my favorite part of writing any book. Having the chance to say thank you to the people who help me in my daily writing life is important and awesome.

Thank you to my writing posse—Kristina, Paula, Kimber, and Amy. Having you ladies in my life makes the downs less painful and the ups more enjoyable. To my critique partner Delphine and her ability to handle my "Mind taking a quick look at this?" texts. My amazing editor, Esi, who always knows exactly where to find the issues and how to fix them. And finally, thank you to my wonderful agent, Courtney. Onward and upward!

Love Christine d'Abo?
Keep an eye out for

30 DAYS

Available now.

And **30 NIGHTS**

Available Summer 2016.

Keep reading for a sneak peek!

"Sexy, fun and deeply emotional. Bravo!"
—J. Kenner, *New York Times* bestselling author

christine d'Abo

What a difference a month makes...

30 days

30 DAYS

So, the thing about me being a widow at the ripe old age of thirty-five was that no one knew what to say or how to act around me. My couple friends still invited me over to their parties, barbecues, and the like, but the conversations always drifted into the land of awkward. *Oh, you look great. I haven't seen you since Rob . . . since the funeral. Did you do something to your hair?*

The few single friends I had tried to pull me into their world. I didn't quite fit with them, though. While they were clubbing or barhopping trying to find the perfect guy, every time I met someone my brain automatically compared him to Rob. I wasn't *still* looking for that special someone—I'd found and lost him.

Being a widow is not quite the same as being divorced. I'd been quite happy being married, having regular, boring sex with my amazing husband, followed by eating cold pizza in bed while we watched the hockey game. It was what I'd always wanted. *He* was who I'd always wanted.

Seriously, fuck cancer.

As a result, I found myself on my own more and more. It wasn't a bad thing, really. I'd been with Rob since I was nineteen and we'd been friends long before we'd officially started dating. We'd grown up together, had the same interests, same fears. Hell, we used to speak in nothing but punch lines, only to dissolve into giggles together when no one else in the room knew what the hell we were talking about.

Not having him by my side had forced me to slowly become a singular entity instead of a plural.

Being on my own was . . . strange. Rob had been gone nearly two years and I still found myself turning to say something to him at the weirdest times. Though over the past month that started happening less frequently. I couldn't tell you exactly how I felt about that. Guilty? Oh my God, yes. But I knew it meant I'd finally started to move on. I hadn't told anyone about my mental shift. Instead, I found myself going to this quiet place in my head, speaking less, observing more. It was different. I guess I'd become different more out of necessity than any real desire to change.

We'd known his time was coming to an end and took the last month of his life to simply enjoy each other. It was on one of our various trips to the beach that he handed me The Envelope.

"What's this?" My fingers were damp from the ocean spray and sticky from the ice cream I'd just finished. "If this is some death letter thing, I can't read it."

He grinned at that. "Naw, it's not sappy or anything. But yes, it's for after I'm gone."

"Rob—"

"Lyssa, listen to me. I promise you it's not what you think." He huffed, puffing out his shallow cheeks. "How many guys have you slept with?" The breeze moved his shirt and the sun made his brown eyes sparkle. If he had any hair left it would have blown from his forehead. My heart ached to run my hands through his hair once more. "And if you say more than one I'll promise not to be pissed."

"Don't be an ass. You know you're the only man I've ever been with." We'd talked a lot about that after we'd gotten married. Rob had a small measure of guilt that I hadn't had a chance to sow my oats. Somehow he thought because of my limited dating experience I would get bored or grow to resent him.

The idiot.

"That's my point." He took my hand and pressed the envelope into my palm once more. "Don't open this until you're ready. Hell, you might not want to open it at all. Just . . ." He gave my hand a squeeze, but for the first time in a long while, he couldn't meet my gaze. "I know you said you didn't think you'd want to be with anyone else."

"I don't." The thought made me ill.

"Baby, you shouldn't be alone. You have too much light and love inside you. The thought of you being on your own, of not having anyone to share in the joy you have to give? No, I know you. There will come a time when you'll realize that you're ready to move on—"

"I won't."

"—and I know you'll feel guilty about that. You'll ignore the feelings for as long as you can, thinking that you don't need anyone. Then something will happen. You'll see someone and in that beautiful brain of yours you'll be all *nice ass, dude,* and that will be it. You'll cry about it, but you'll realize you're ready."

"Please. I wouldn't cry." Because it wouldn't happen. Ever. "Not over a nice ass."

He chuckled, finally looking me in the eye. "You'll cry. But then you'll remember this conversation and know that I was right. So, I'm going to say *I told you so* now. Then I want you to take this envelope and open it."

"Rob—"

"It's about sex."

I stood there with my mouth open. "What?"

"Just some ideas I had for you about sex when I'm gone. Getting back on the horse. Riding the cowboy. That sort of thing."

I wasn't ready to think about him being gone, let alone wanting to have sex with someone else. "I don't want to talk about this anymore. Seriously, shut up or I'm going to punch you."

"Okay."

He didn't let me forget about the envelope. He tried to get me to talk about it, but I would always cut him off. When I shoved it into a pile of papers in the closet, it found its way back onto my dresser. That box in the basement of papers that was older than me? Materialized on top of my desk. The recycling bin? Back onto the counter. I could have continued to play that game, but then Rob took another turn for the worse and all thoughts of envelopes and what they contained were the last things on my mind.

The cancer won.

And I was suddenly alone.

It really wasn't as bad as I'd first assumed it would be. I thought a lot about Rob and missed him terribly for the better part of the first year. I functioned, worked, went out, but that was more of an automated response than actual living. There'd been more tears than I ever thought possible. My chest ached and my stomach churned. When I didn't feel ill, my mind wandered. I couldn't pretend to have any focus. My friends and the people at work never called me on my distraction.

Then I started to emerge from under the darkness and began to live once more. I still missed Rob, thought about him daily, but the tightness in my chest eased. That's when the guilt kicked in. At least he'd already told me it would.

I stopped going out to our friends' homes for a while. They'd begun to get used to me as a singular—Alyssa—and not a plural—Rob and Alyssa. With their ease came my anger that they were all still couples. Their lives hadn't been shattered and swept away without their permission. They'd smile, laugh, and all the while I wanted to scream at them.

So, I stayed away.

It helped. I was able to catch my breath, cry, hit things, and slowly my brain adjusted. I could be allowed into public once more, no longer a danger to happy couples.

One thing that helped was changing up my routine. I'd rearranged all the furniture in our condo, painted the walls, even put up some new pictures. Rob would have hated them. I wasn't a fan myself, but it served its purpose. I started going to a new coffee shop half a block farther away from our building. I saw new people as I went, had to train a new barista named Len, smiled at a street performer who always played the same three songs on his guitar. It was good.

By the time the beginning of June rolled around, the tension had bled from my shoulders. It had taken me nearly two years, but I knew I was going to be okay.

That was when it happened.

A new guy moved into the complex.

Our building was a renovated school, each unit composed of three converted classrooms. Rob loved that we had a working water fountain just outside our front door. For fun, we'd mentally labeled the condos by classes. We were English because of the sheer number of books we had. Mr. and Mrs. Le Page were French, the Chin family were Home Ec, and on and on. The new guy had moved into Tourism, the condo owned by some company that let their out-of-town employees stay there for extended periods of time. It was just down the hall on the side opposite our place.

No, *my* place.

And he had a nice ass.

I knew this because my first sight of him was him bent over, pushing a large box through his front door. His jeans were stretched tight as his long legs worked against their load. I don't know how long I stood there, but it was enough that I hadn't unlocked my front door and he must have felt my gaze on him. He looked over his shoulder and smiled.

My body shivered. Even with the distance between us, I felt the intensity of his gaze.

Then I heard Rob's chuckle in my brain, that little one he'd give me when he knew he'd won an argument. I had to get in before I looked even more the idiot. I waved to the guy and immediately fumbled with my key. I knew he was watching me, which made the entire process of opening the door a monumental task. *Click, whoosh, bang* and I was safely inside. I pressed my forehead to the door and contemplated the probability of dying from embarrassment. Given my current state, upward of forty percent chance of death.

The bastard *did* have a nice ass.

It was in that moment that I remembered my conversation with Rob at the beach and his envelope. I was guilty, but that guilt wasn't nearly as strong as it had once been. With my hand pressed against the wood, I pushed away and slowly made my way to the bedroom. The envelope had taken up residence in my underwear drawer—I knew Rob would approve—deep beneath my panties and socks. I hadn't thought about it for quite some time, but rather than feel sad about the prospect of opening it, I had a strange tingle of anticipation.

I held it in my hands as I sat on the edge of the bed. The stains from my ice cream–coated fingers were still on the envelope. Chocolate with fudge. I ran my thumb across them.

Nothing else adorned the front of the envelope, no indication of what may be inside. I huffed, then licked my lips before I finally slipped my finger beneath the edge and tore the paper open.

30 NIGHTS

"You are the biggest coward in the world."

Yup, that's me—Glenna Marie O'Donald—stellar research assistant and consummate romantic coward.

Jasmine, my best friend since my first year of college, fell into the chair opposite me at our table in the lunchroom. I wasn't bothered by her comments; she was right, after all. My history with guys was shaky at best. I liked them and they seemed to like me for a time. Then inevitably things devolved when my job took priority over hanging out.

Your boss is taking advantage of you.

You work way too much.

Why can't you spend as much time with me as you do at the school?

This sucks. I'm out of here.

Honestly, when you get burned more than a few times for the same thing, you tend to back away. I didn't *need* a man in my life. Jasmine never believed me when I told her that I was quite happy on my own. She'd snort, roll her eyes, and wave away my comment without a second glance.

It did get annoying.

I *didn't* need a man.

Even if I sometimes wanted someone special in my life. Occasionally. Every so often.

"I'm telling you, the staff barbecue is the perfect place for you to talk to him." She opened her lunch and the smell of kimchi rice filled the room.

The *him* she was referring to was Professor Eric Morris. The tall, dark-haired, super-fit sociology professor had a voice that could melt hearts and drop panties with a simple *hello*. Professor Eric Morris, who had more female students in his class than anyone else on campus. A man who rarely smiled, but when he looked at you there was no doubt he not only saw you, but every thought and feeling that flitted through your head. He starred in far too many of my nightly fantasies for me to admit without sounding like a crazy, obsessed stalker.

The man, who in the year and a bit that he'd been teaching at the college, I'd barely managed to say two words to, because I was, as Jasmine put it, a coward.

"I love you like a sister, Jaz. But there is no way I'm going to say anything to him. Ever."

It was the Friday before the Labor Day weekend, the last work day before the start of the school year. Most of the professors from the college were gone, taking their last bit of vacation to play golf, read, or whatever their passions happened to be. I loved working this time of year. The school was quiet. It always felt as though someone had taken a deep breath and were waiting to exhale. A collective pause before the chaos to come.

This year was going to be especially awesome. Professor Mickelson, my boss, had already been away for three months on his semester-long sabbatical. I still had four more months of only communicating with him via e-mail. Heaven!

"Are you insane?" Jasmine threw her napkin at me. "This is the perfect time for you to do it. He'll be there. You'll be there. Your crazy boss *won't* be there. You might even be able to relax and have fun for once."

She was my best friend in the whole wide world, but there were times when Jasmine scared the shit out of me. I looked down at my hands and picked at the dry skin around my nail. "I just can't."

"What's the worst that can happen? He'll say no. At the very least you'll have an answer and you can move on to someone else."

A grad student chose that moment to come into the kitchen. He didn't even look at us as he made his way to the coffee machine. I leaned forward to close the distance between me and Jasmine. "I'm quite happy with my fantasies, thank you."

"I bet you are. I bet you dream about climbing up his body and licking every inch of his skin."

The grad student looked at us wide-eyed before he spun away quickly. I got the impression he was still listening, no doubt wanting to get some dirt that could be passed around the student lounge. Great, like I need *that* kind of attention.

I nodded my head in the direction of our friend. "Can you keep your voice down a bit?"

"Not if you're not going to listen to my advice." She leaned back and crossed her arms, her eyes locked onto mine. "You need to make a move before someone else snatches him up."

Now the grad student wasn't even pretending that he wasn't paying attention. Jasmine must have picked up on it, too, because in the next instant she turned around and glared at him. "Don't you have someplace to be, Stuart? Like running your tutorial?"

"Ah, yeah. Yes." For a moment I thought his eyes were going to bug out of his head.

"Then move your ass." Jasmine pointed at the door and narrowed her gaze.

I'd never seen a person move that quickly before in my life.

When she turned her glare back on me, I knew I wasn't going to be spared anything. "Glenna, I know you don't believe me, but this is the truth. You are not meant to be alone. You and Eric would be cute together. He's serious, you're serious. Just think about what sex would be like with him. Jesus, if I weren't gay, even I'd be tempted to take him for a ride myself."

And there was a mental picture I so didn't want—my best friend and my crush fucking.

"I hate you." I pulled my tuna sandwich out of my container and took a giant bite. "He doesn't even know I'm alive. Saying hello to him at the barbecue isn't going to do anything to help get him into my bed."

"Well, you can't expect him to fuck you if you can't at least have a simple conversation." She took a big bite of her kimchi and waved her fork around. "Maybe you can get drunk and then grope his ass. Then you'd have to go apologize. There might be groveling. 'Oh, please, Eric, how can I ever make it up to you?'" She batted her eyelashes at me before laughing. "You should see your face."

"You're an asshole. Why are we even friends?"

"Because I showed you how to shotgun a beer our first week of college."

"Only after I saved your ass with that essay."

But as she knew, my brain does this thing that as soon as someone puts a thought out there, I can't help but picture how things will work out, all the way to their natural conclusion. In my head I saw myself at the party. Eric would walk by on his way to the food table or something. I'd "accidentally" bump into him as he passed me and look into his eyes all surprised. Maybe I'd even spill a drink on myself. He'd think he'd done it and would help me clean myself.

I'm sorry, Glenna. How can I make up for this?

Oh, nothing. It was an accident.

I can't stand by while I've done you wrong. At least let me give you a clean shirt.

I'd blush, of course, because who wouldn't. *Thank you.*

Why don't you take mine? His voice would be that low rumble that always seemed to turn me on. His eyes would be locked onto me as he'd slowly unbutton his shirt.

Wow, Eric. Your chest is so firm.

Would you like to see the rest of me?

And bam, crazy-monkey sex!

If only.

I cleared my throat and quickly took another bite of my sandwich. "I don't think Eric likes anyone. Or has sex. Or anything. He's always on his own."

"Baby, I've seen that man. He's having sex. As much as he wants with whomever he wants to do it with. I keep telling you all you need to do is go after him."

"He doesn't know I'm alive," I said again. And I was essentially a coworker. That went against so many things on my mental *don't touch list* I couldn't fathom it.

"Whose fault is that? Not his. If you want someone, then you need to do something about it. Life doesn't reward the cautious."

"Sometimes it does."

"You don't believe that."

I hated when she was right. "Maybe."

"You're a research assistant who lives in the world of studies and observations. Talk to him—hell, I was serious about the groping. I'm sure you could chalk this up to some exceptionally hands-on research project."

"God, you're a child sometimes. I don't need a man to fulfill me when I have a perfectly good vibrator at home to help—"

"Baby, all you do is masturbate."

"—live out my fantasies. I'd be scared that the reality would never live up to the imaginary Eric that I've created in my head."

It was in that moment that my skin began to tingle. We were still alone in the kitchen, but I could have sworn someone was there. It was probably Stuart standing outside in the hall trying to get some more dirt. Well, he was out of luck because I was done being brow-beaten by Jasmine.

"I need to get back soon. Professor Mickelson left me a pile of books to pull and outline for him. He'll be chasing me through e-mails if I'm not done soon."

Thankfully, she sighed, signaling the end of her teasing. "When does the old goat get back?"

"He's off all term, but he's threatened to come back around the end of October for a check-in. Then I'm sure he'll have me buried in another bunch of new projects before the next term starts."

"I'd better head out too. I have a one-thirty meeting. Apparently the computer science profs want to do a study on online learning again. I have to pull some old case studies so they don't rehash an old thesis."

"Blah."

The echo of our chairs scraping as we stood filled the room. One second I was picking up my garbage and taking it to the garbage can, and in the next I was face-to-face with the object of my lust.

Professor Eric Morris stood in the doorway, coffee mug in hand. Well, *stood* isn't quite the right description. It's more like he *loomed*. He's probably only a smidgen over six feet tall, but being only five foot four myself, it makes for a huge difference from my perspective. Mind you, being eye level with his chest was no hardship. His dress shirts fit him perfectly, but they couldn't hide the muscles beneath. As usual, I was paying more attention to his pecs—were they really as firm as they looked?—rather than his face. That was why I didn't immediately notice him staring at me. Which he totally was.

And there was my blush. "Umm, hi, Professor Morris."

Woot, go me! I finally spoke to him.

"Glenna."

God, his voice! It was a lot lower than any other man that I knew, and it had a way of seeping into my body when he spoke. Could the sound of a voice be an aphrodisiac? If so, then I could listen to him read the phone book and probably have an orgasm.

Jasmine cleared her throat and I realized that we'd been standing staring at each other for longer than was normal. I looked at the garbage in my hand and then at the garbage can directly behind him. "Umm, sorry. I just need to . . ."

I'd half expected him to move to the side so I could reach it. Instead, he stayed put, forcing me to step awkwardly around him. I clamped my mouth closed as I moved so he wouldn't be subjected to the stench of my tuna breath. As I brushed past him, I got a nose full of his aftershave. It wasn't a brand that I knew, but he smelled awesome and it always made me a bit giddy when he was nearby. I could always tell when he'd been in a room, my nose keenly aware of his lingering scent.

It was only after I finally dropped my garbage into the bin that Eric moved over to the coffee machines. I wasn't a close colleague to him and hadn't worked on any of his projects since he'd come to the school, so I didn't have much I could say to him. Not that he was particularly easy to speak to with his back to us. I scampered over to the table and grabbed my things. "I need to stop and get some paper for my printer."

"Cool." Jasmine was clearly trying to fight off a laughing fit. "Want to grab a coffee before we go? You look like you could use one."

I'm going to kill her. "No, I'm good for now."

Just before we left the kitchen, Jasmine piped up. "Have a great day, Professor Morris."

"You as well, Ms. Houng, Glenna."

Yes, she was going to die in the most painful way possible.

Somehow I managed to keep my mouth shut until we were out of earshot. "I hate you."

"Are you kidding me? For a second I thought he was going to throw you over the table and fuck you in front of me."

"You're high. He doesn't know me."

"Don't be so dramatic. He knew your name, which means he

knows who you are. And you couldn't see his face the way I did. Not only does that boy know you're alive, but he's interested."

"Whatever." She was just trying to get me going. He couldn't be interested.

As we were about to turn the corner, I looked back down the hall toward the kitchen. Eric was standing there, coffee cup in his hand, staring back at me.

Photo by Mark Arsenault

Christine d'Abo is a romance novelist and short story writer, with more than thirty publications to her name. She loves to exercise and she stops writing just long enough to keep her body in motion too. When she's not pretending to be a ninja in her basement, she's most likely spending time with husband, daughters, and her two dogs.